THE CAT WHO LOVED DAVID DUCHOVNY

JAMES BLAKEY

WHITAKER LYON PRESS

Broadway, Virginia

Contents

Dedication   V

Epigraph   VII

The Cat Who Loved David Duchovny   1

The Witch of Sherman Oaks   21

The Last Mission   49

About the Author   97

For Ghork, the best cat ever.

"I believe cats to be spirits come to Earth. A cat, I am sure, could walk on a cloud without coming through."

Jules Verne

The Cat Who Loved David Duchovny

YIP! ARF! VOOV!

A grouchy Madame Marie Curie cracked open a sleepy eye. In the park across the street, a brown-and-white dog soared into the air, snatched a neon green Frisbee with its jaws, and tumbled to the ground. The beagle bounded back to his owner and presented her with the trophy. Slobbering on the grass, the dog received a pat on the head for his accomplishment. The beagle's red-headed owner launched the disc again. Frisbee Dog raced after its prey, barking all the way.

<u>Dogs! They have no sense of shame.</u>

Marie's perfect lazing spot in the sunbeam ruined by the ongoing canine antics, she leapt from her windowsill perch. The two-bedroom apartment provided plenty of distractions to occupy her time. She raced from Jim's bedroom to the living room, vaulted over the ottoman, and skidded to a stop atop the glass coffee table.

With her dark brown paw, the blue-point Siamese batted the remote and depressed the power button. The fifty-inch high-definition screen, surrounded on all sides by packed bookshelves, blinked to life.

Marie extended her claws, depressing buttons and navigating the streaming service menus. The opening credits from *The X-Files* rolled. As the haunting theme played, Marie jumped to the royal blue sectional sofa, kneaded her spot, and curled up next to a cushion.

Special Agent Fox Mulder! Eyes soft and brown as Tastee-Kat treats. That's a man I'd let rub my tummy and scratch my ears.

Not that Jim wasn't a good guy. Warm and snuggly in bed. But Jim was no David Duchovny!

Marie watched with rapt attention whenever Fox appeared or spoke. She'd yawn and close her eyes when Agent Scully was on the screen.

"I'm home," Jim announced.

Marie glanced in the direction of the door for the briefest of moments, before returning to her show.

"*X-Files* again?" Jim rubbed under Marie's chin. "This is a good one. It's got Cigarette Smoking Man in it."

Jim reclined on the sofa. Marie climbed into his lap to watch the show together.

Jim stroked her. "Who has the softest fur?"

You know it. Marie purred.

When the credits rolled, Jim turned off the TV. "That's enough for today. I need a shower. We're having company, and you need to be on your best behavior." He wagged his finger at Marie.

Marie swatted at Jim's finger and tried to bite it.

"And no biting Debbie."

Marie's ears perked up.

"That's right, a lady friend from work is coming over. I'm cooking dinner. I'm nervous enough and don't need you adding stress."

Jim stood, forcing Marie from his vanishing lap. She climbed on the back of the sofa watching Jim disappear into his bedroom.

<u>Lady friend? Better not be another Lauren with her laugh like a demented mockingbird.</u>

As the sound of the running shower filled the apartment, Marie turned the television back on increasing the volume to drown out the noise.

Twenty minutes later, Jim emerged from his bedroom. He wore a dress shirt and slacks, hair combed, freshly shaved, and drenched in that awful cologne that reminded Marie of the vet's office. Jim frowned at the TV, killed the power, and placed the remote on the highest bookshelf, far out of the range of Marie's jumping ability.

"I said no more television. I'm going to make dinner. Come to the kitchen if you want something."

Marie grumpily padded after Jim. He refreshed the water dish and dumped a cup of food into her bowl. As she crunched her dry (some mediocre food scientist's idea of what salmon should taste like), the scent of raw chicken filled the air. She leapt to the granite countertop to investigate.

"No." Jim shook his finger at her. He picked up Marie with one hand and dropped her to the floor.

She immediately returned to the counter.

"This is people food."

Marie lowered her head, making sad eyes at Jim.

Jim sighed. "Okay, you get one little piece and that's it." He sliced off a bit of chicken. "If you don't behave after that, it's off to the guest room."

Marie scarfed down the meat, dove for the floor, and filled her tummy with dry. She returned to the living room, hopping into her three-story cat condo set in the corner adjacent to the computer desk. The smell of chicken parmesan, her favorite, filled the apartment. As she drifted off to sleep, she promised herself that no matter what Jim said or did, she would enjoy some of his dinner.

***

The buzzer sounded, jolting Marie awake. Jim rushed to the door. Debbie had bright blond hair like the sun. Her short black skirt left plenty of tanned flesh exposed, a perfect target for Marie's claws. She shuddered at the sight of Debbie's dangerously high heels. Getting her tail caught under those spikes would not be fun.

Jim gawked at Debbie.

"Aren't you going to invite me in?" Debbie flashed her smile, displaying dazzling white teeth.

"Uh, sure. Please come in." Jim backed up, almost stumbling over his feet.

Marie strolled across the room, looked up at the newcomer, and announced herself.

Miaw!

"This is Marie. Short for Madame Marie Curie.

Debbie reached down to pet her. Marie found herself engulfed by Debbie's perfume, a powerful floral aroma tickling her nose.

Kerchoo!

Debbie giggled. "How cute. The kitty is sneezing!"

Kitty? Watch your step, Blondie!

"Have a seat on the sofa. I'll get you a glass of wine. Dinner will be ready in about ten minutes."

He walked back to the kitchen with a goofy grin on his face. Marie had seen Jim like this before; it was never a good sign.

Instead of sitting, Debbie wandered about the living room, inspecting the bookshelves. She spotted Jim's walnut computer desk, scrutinized the PC sitting under it, and nodded.

Debbie dropped her purse on the coffee table and stood to the side of the doorway between the living room and kitchen. As Jim emerged, she stepped into his path, bumping him. Red wine spilt all over his shirt.

"Gosh, I'm so sorry!" Debbie said. "Let me get something to clean that up."

"It's okay." Jim handed her the glass. "I'll go change."

As Jim's bedroom door closed, Debbie put down her drink. She removed a USB stick from her purse, walked to Jim's computer desk, and knelt.

Espionage! Like when David guest-starred in *The Lone Gunmen.*

Like a lion stalking her prey on the African savannah, Marie crept across the living room. Debbie was inches away from inserting the stick into an open port, when Marie attacked and bit her hand.

Debbie cried and dropped the stick. Marie scooped it up with her mouth, scampering away. Debbie chased after her. As Marie crossed the threshold into the kitchen, Debbie yanked her tail.

Miaw!

In shock, Marie dropped the stick. She swatted it with her paw. The stick skidded across the tile floor, sliding into the tiny gap beneath the refrigerator.

Debbie shoved Marie out of the way, bent in front of the fridge, and slipped her fingers underneath. Too narrow. She pressed her head to the floor, closed one eye, and squinted. Nothing but shadows.

"Thanks a lot, *Kitty*."

You're welcome, Blondie.

"What's going on?" Jim appeared in the doorway, wearing a fresh blue dress shirt.

"We were just playing." Debbie reached to pet Marie, but the cat hissed, hair standing on end, and rushed from the room.

"I'm sorry," Jim said. "Sometimes she's standoffish around new people."

"It's okay, I prefer us to be alone." Debbie stood, stepped close to Jim, and traced a finger across his chest. "I see you working in Special Projects and wonder what you're up to in there all day long."

Jim half-grinned. "Well, we're really not allowed to discuss it. Even with folks from other departments."

Debbie looped her arms around Jim's neck and pulled her body against his. She whispered, her hot breath in his ear, "Oh, you can tell me. Or maybe later we can play Interrogator and Captive." She kissed his neck.

The oven timer beeped.

"I've got to get that." Jim extracted himself from Debbie's embrace. "Table's set. I'll be right out with dinner."

Debbie frowned to herself and went to sit down.

On a bookshelf, Marie perched like a gargoyle, her tail swishing with contempt. Jim brought out dinner, nervously setting the dishes on the table and constantly asking Debbie if everything were all right.

"This is delicious." Debbie swallowed a bit of chicken parmesan. "You are an amazing cook."

"It's not that difficult." Jim blushed slightly. "Cooking is just applied chemistry."

"I love the garlic broccolini. And did you bake your own bread?"

"Guilty as char—"

Marie leapt on the table, attempting to steal Jim's chicken. With a backhand, he sent her falling to the floor.

Jim frowned. "I don't know what's got into her this evening."

"Don't worry about the kitty," Debbie said. "So how does your knowledge of chemistry help you in the kitchen? Is it related at all to what Special Projects is working on?"

"Not really," Jim said. "But what about your job in Marketing? I'd like to hear about that."

Debbie gulped her wine. "Social media. Trade shows. Customer engagement. It's all so terribly dull." She shook her head. "But what you guys are up to on the fourth floor? Now that sounds interes—"

Miaw!

Marie jumped on the table, taking another run at the chicken. Jim blocked her assault with an elbow, then used both hands to push her off the table with more force than necessary. She skulked across the room, climbed into her cat condo, and pouted.

When the couple finished with the meal, Jim rose to clear the table.

"Don't worry about the dishes," Debbie said. "Bring more wine and sit with me on the sofa."

Jim returned from the kitchen with a glass for Debbie, grabbed the remote from the high bookshelf, and took a seat. He tapped the remote; lights dimmed and music played.

"Impressive," Debbie said.

"Universal remote. I wired up the entire apartment."

"Clever." Debbie slid down the sofa, pressing herself against Jim. "So, what is it you guys do in the lab all day?"

Jim shook his head. "I told you, we're all sworn to secrecy."

"Don't be such a boy scout." Debbie traced a finger across his cheek, down to his chin, then across his lips. She slipped off a shoe and ran her foot against his leg.

This display was enough to make Marie want to hack up a hairball. She grudgingly conceded Debbie passed for what was considered attractive with her long hair and even longer legs. Combined with the wine, the perfume, and the mood, Jim was clearly succumbing to her charms.

"I guess it can't hurt to give you a broad outline of what we're working on," Jim said. "Special Projects has developed a new battery prototype that can store close to fifty times more energy than the existing technology."

Debbie fiddled with his collar. "That's amazing. Was it your breakthrough?"

"We're a team. Simmons came up with the idea to use Cadmium G—"

"Argh!" Debbie flinched in pain.

"What's wrong?" Jim asked.

"Your cat!" Debbie lifted her leg. Her shin dripped with blood.

"I'll get you a towel." Jim ran off.

Marie hopped onto the coffee table and glared at Debbie. Debbie swung her hand at the cat, but Marie dodged it and scampered away.

Jim returned with the towel, Bactine, and some bandages.

Debbie mopped up the blood. She grimaced as Jim sprayed the antiseptic. She applied the bandages and stood. "I think I should leave, Jim. I'd be happy to see you again." She glared at Marie, who watched from the second level of the cat condo. "But next time, I suggest we go out for dinner." She grabbed her purse, stormed across the room, and slammed the door.

Jim grabbed Marie with both hands and held her face close to his. "Why do you have to be so jealous?"

Marie stared into Jim's blue eyes, willing him to understand.

<u>She's a spy! I saved you before you spilled the beans.</u>

"I hope a night in the guest room will improve your attitude." Jim carried her to the spare bedroom and tossed the cat on the bed. He returned with the litter box and slammed the door.

Marie curled up on a pillow and sulked.

I bet this never happens to David Duchovny's cat.

***

Marie woke to sunlight filtering through the blinds. She arched her back and stretched. The door was open; her punishment over. She padded to the kitchen where she found Jim and rubbed against his leg.

"Good morning. No hard feelings?" He held two Tastee-Kat treats in the palm of his hand.

Tuna!

Marie gobbled them up.

Jim filled her bowl, refreshed the water, and scratched her ears. "Off to work. See you tonight."

Marie's busy day consisted of napping on Jim's bed, on the guest bed, in her cat condo, and on the sofa. At noon, she finished what was left in her bowl, then lay on the windowsill until Frisbee Dog made his raucous reappearance. She investigated a noise she hoped could be a mouse but turned out to be the refrigerator compressor. She munched on a couple of plant leaves and washed herself three times. To finish the day, she enjoyed a David Duchovny double feature: *Playing God* and *Evolution*, before falling asleep again.

She woke to the sound of Jim talking on his phone.

"Sure Debbie, how about Dagastino's? It's around the corner from my place." He paused. "Great, I'll see you there in twenty minutes."

Marie glared at Jim.

"Don't give me that attitude." Jim disappeared into his bedroom.

The shower ran for a few minutes, and he emerged wearing a sports coat and tie. Marie raced up to him, wrapped her front paws around his shin, and bit him.

"Stop that!" Jim picked up Marie with both hands.

<u>Debbie can't be trusted.</u>

"It looks like you earned another trip to the guest room." He dumped Marie on the bed and slammed the door. A few seconds later, Marie heard the front door closing and the lock turning.

She couldn't believe Jim would be so foolish as to be taken in by Debbie. Marie needed to protect him, but how? She leapt off the bed, padded to the door, stood on her back legs, and stretched. The doorknob was out of reach.

Marie jumped to the windowsill. The window was up, only the screen between her and the outside world. The lower right was deformed, the metal wires ripped, forming a hole. But too small for her. She pressed her nose into the opening and pushed.

Rawr!

The tiny metal wires slashed at her face, but the hole widened a bit. She extended her claws, catching them in the tiny metallic openings, and pulled. Then she forced her face into the hole again. Ten minutes of slicing and pushing created an opening wide enough to squeeze through. This would be the first time Marie had been outside. Being in a carrier to and from the vet didn't count.

She pushed through the screen and found herself on a ledge in the shadows. A light breeze brushed her whiskers. She peered over the side; she was three stories high. How to get down? She followed the ledge and turned a corner. A tree branch extended toward the building, but not all the way. She'd have to jump.

Marie remembered that cliffhanger in season three when Agent Mulder leapt from a bridge onto a passing train. David Duchovny did his own stunts in that episode. If he could do it, so could she.

Marie crouched and shifted her weight to her hind legs. Her tail wiggled as she studied the gap between the ledge and the branch. She contracted her thigh muscles, then exploded, launching into the air.

Marie caught the branch with her front paws. For a moment she dangled over the sidewalk, then pulled herself up. With perfect balance, she walked to the trunk of the tree, maneuvered downward through the thick maze of branches, and dropped to the ground.

The city was filled with noises: cars honking, radios blaring, people shouting. And the smells: garbage, rubber, oil! The pavement was covered with splotches of long discarded chewing gum. She longed for the peace and cleanliness of Jim's apartment.

Marie winced as she pattered along the sidewalk. Her paws weren't used to the rough surface. She stopped at an intersection. Was Jim on the next block? She wasn't thrilled with the idea of crossing the street. A large black truck, its engine rattling like a machine gun, raced by emitting a black cloud of smoke. Marie coughed and darted away. Out of the corner of her eye, she spotted Jim.

He sat with Debbie at a table on a patio. Debbie laughed at something he said and placed her hand on Jim's forearm.

Marie prowled toward the table. She crawled into a bush that afforded a view of the pair and formulated a plan. If Jim were to see her, he'd take her back to the apartment and make sure she couldn't get out again. That would only delay Debbie. Marie needed to permanently remove her from Jim's life.

Jim stood. Was he leaving? No, he didn't head toward the exit to the sidewalk. He went the other way and disappeared into the restaurant. Debbie pulled a vial filled with blue liquid from her purse, dumped the contents into Jim's glass, and stirred with the straw.

<u>Poison!</u>

Marie needed to save Jim. Now! Knock over the glass and figure out the rest later. Marie crept out of her hiding spot, right into the face of Frisbee Dog.

The beagle attempted to lick her. Marie hissed. She circled past the dog. The beagle yipped and lurched forward. The leash slipped from the owner's hand. Frisbee Dog was loose, chasing Marie.

Marie dashed away from the restaurant, darting between pedestrians. The yelping dog barreled down the sidewalk in hot pursuit. A teenager on a skateboard came within inches of rolling over Marie's tail. She leapt on a newspaper dispenser and from there to the top of a mailbox. Her hair on end, too out of breath to hiss, she arched her back and bared her teeth. The dog stood on its back legs, using the mailbox for support, and howled at Marie, but she was out of reach.

The owner caught up with the dog. Admonishing him, she grabbed the leash, dragging the beagle away. Marie caught her breath and hissed until Frisbee Dog vanished from sight. She closed her eyes and let her fur relax.

<u>Jim!</u>

She leapt to the ground and dashed to the restaurant. Jim was standing, supported by Debbie. A look of distress and confusion on his face.

"If you're not feeling well, maybe I should take you back to your place." Debbie led him slowly along the sidewalk toward his building.

<u>I have to get home first.</u>

Marie ran to the tree, scaling it to the branch that approached to the building. The farther she advanced, the more the branch sagged. She stopped when it became too narrow. The jump appeared longer than last time. But she did it before, she could do it again.

Marie readied herself: hocks bent, weight back, muscles contracted. She launched, but her front paws bounced off the ledge. She slammed into the side of the building and tumbled toward the ground.

Instinctively, Marie bent her body in the middle, tucked her front legs in, extended her rear legs, and rotated the front half of her body. Then she did the opposite: extending her front legs, tucking in her rear legs, and rotating her back half.

Marie righted herself before passing the second floor. She spread her legs, landing in the hedge surrounding the building.

Miaw!

Scratched and dazed, Marie extricated herself from the dense branches, licked her wounds, then rushed to the building entrance. She slipped in the double doors as a man in a fedora exited. She dashed up the steps to the third floor to see Debbie leading Jim out of the elevator.

Debbie had Jim's keys in her hand. She fiddled with the lock and opened the door. Marie slipped in behind them.

Debbie led the compliant Jim to his computer desk and dropped him in the chair. He sat motionless; his eyes glazed over. She powered on the PC.

<u>Must stop Debbie!</u>

Last winter the electricity went out when Jim plugged in the Christmas tree while everything else was on. With Debbie's back to the coffee table, Marie leaped on the table and pressed the buttons on the remote madly, powering on every device and light in the apartment.

The TV roared to life, and Debbie turned. "Stop that." She pulled a gun from her purse, pointed it at Marie, and took a step toward her.

The apartment plunged into darkness. In the dark, Debbie couldn't see her, but Marie could see Debbie. Marie scampered off the table, circled around, and hid in the cat condo.

Debbie retrieved her phone from her purse, adding slight illumination to the room, and made a call.

"I'm at Cooley's place, but the power is out. I can't grab any data from his PC." She paused. "Long story." She paused again. "Okay, I'll snatch the tower and his phone. Do you want me to interrogate him? I gave him a dose of the blue; he's malleable." Another pause. "I'll try that and meet you back at the hotel."

Debbie activated her flashlight app and shone it on Jim. She slipped her hand into Jim's front left pocket and pulled out his wallet. She tossed it aside. From his front right pocket, she retrieved his phone. As she slid it into her purse, Marie, claws extended, leapt from her hiding spot and tore into her hand.

"Aiiiee! Stupid cat!" Both phones fell to the carpet.

Marie pushed and swatted Jim's phone around the corner of the sofa. Debbie shone her phone around the room, but couldn't find Marie.

Marie didn't know Jim's unlock code. With her claws she clicked the emergency call link.

"Nine One One. Police, fire, or ambulance?" the operator said.

"Aha! Got you." Debbie lunged at the cat.

Marie swatted the phone, and it skidded under the sofa. She raced out of Debbie's reach. She jumped on the computer desk, knocking Debbie's purse over and spilling its contents on the floor.

Debbie gathered her belongings back into the purse. She got on her knees and worked furiously to disconnect all the peripherals and cords from the PC tower. Marie extended her claws and sliced the back of her Debbie's exposed legs.

Debbie screamed. She reached for the gun and tried to swat Marie with it. Marie crawled under the coffee table. Debbie returned to the PC and finished disconnecting the cables.

She caressed Jim's cheek. "Sorry lover, can't hang around to pump you for secrets. This will have to do." She held the PC under one arm and grabbed her purse with the other. She opened the door, stepping into the hall.

Marie, belly low to the floor, slunk behind her.

In the hall, Debbie stepped into the path of a police officer.

"Good evening, ma'am," he said. "We received a call from this apartment. Is everything all right?"

"Yes, Officer. Just a misdial." Debbie flashed a smile that was all teeth. She tried to close the door, but Marie stood in the way, yelping when the door struck her. The door remained ajar.

"Is this your apartment?" the cop asked.

"Actually, it belongs to a friend."

"Is your friend home now?"

"No, he lent me his keys. He asked me to fix his computer." She nodded at the tower.

Marie hissed at Debbie, then rubbed against the cop's leg.

"Looks like your friend's cat got out," the cop said.

Debbie kicked at Marie. "Go back inside."

Marie hid behind the cop.

"Let's look inside your *friend's* apartment." The cop unsnapped his holster, placing his hand on the gun's grip. He reached inside and flipped the switch. "Why don't the lights work?"

"I think a fuse blew," Debbie said.

Marie dashed between the cop's legs and over to Jim. She bit him on the leg.

Jim moaned.

The cop pulled a flashlight from his belt and shone it on Jim. "Put down that computer, Lady. You've got some explaining to do."

Miaw!

Marie smugly swished her tail at Debbie.

***

Marie scrolled through the online menus, stopping on the logo for *Stargate SG-1*. She hit play. The rousing theme boomed from the speakers, filling the apartment. Richard Dean Anderson's face flashed on the screen.

<u>Colonel Jack O'Neill! I'd like to eat treats from his hand.</u> <u>He's not at all like that horrible, two-timing David Duchovny. Poor Téa Leoni. She deserved much better.</u>

Marie closed her eyes, falling asleep to the sounds of Colonel O'Neill barking orders and cracking wise. She woke when Jim came home and sat on the couch.

"What are you watching? *MacGyver*? Oh, *Stargate*. I don't think I've seen this one." Jim scratched under her chin, and she purred in return.

Near the end of the episode, the door buzzer sounded.

Jim paused the show. "I'm expecting a new friend."

Marie's ears perked up.

"Don't worry. She's not at all like Debbie."

Jim headed to the door, Marie padding behind him. He opened the door to reveal the redhead from the park. And Frisbee Dog! The beagle dropped the slobber-laden disc on the carpet, stepped up to Marie, and licked her. Jim and the redhead erupted in laughter.

Miaw!

Marie made a face and swatted the dog on the nose. With her eyes, she pleaded at Jim.

Spies and dog owners! Why can't you date a respectable woman?

THE END

The Witch of Sherman Oaks

"Why can't you just turn Jason into a frog?" Boise Davenport frowned, brushing back a loose strand of her unnaturally red hair.

We were sitting in my living room, which was doubling as my office, as business was slow.

"That's not the sort of thing I do. No matter how much someone might deserve it," I said. *Why does everyone always want a frog?*

Boise (real name Janet Kretzel) hit it big on one of those reality shows where the producers strand you in the tropics with little in the way of clothing. By the end of the first episode, #RedBoise was trending.

She was attempting to parley that popularity into an acting career but her big break was being held up by an intransigent casting director who she implied was a candidate for #MeToo. Hence the amphibious transformation request.

Boise removed her over-sized sunglasses, revealing green eyes with a conspiratorial bent. "Not necessarily a frog. A badger or a groundhog would do. It doesn't even have to be an animal. Just something to get him out of the way. Make him allergic to Wi-Fi and he'll have to move to the woods in West Virginia." She smiled at me with perfect white teeth. Those caps must have set her back at least ten grand.

I shook my head. "In my practice, I like to be constructive. Build up my clients, rather than tear down others."

"What about that Supreme Court Justice you put a hex on?" She pointed to the blown up, framed cover of *LA Magazine* hanging on the wall. A professional hair and make-up job and the talents of a skilled Photoshop artist resulted in the Platonic Ideal of myself above the caption "Meet the Face of the #NewResistance: Jennifer Griffiths is The Witch of Sherman Oaks."

At Polliwog Park the day before the confirmation vote, I burned sage, coriander, dandelion roots, and a photo of Smirking Judge Punchable Face in a silver chalice, while I danced and chanted a curse that my Welsh grandmother taught me. So many crazy things happen in LA every day, but my video went viral. The raccoon carrying her babies in the background might have helped. I was in *Variety*, *Deadline*, and interviewed by Don Lemon on CNN.

I shrugged. "You'll notice he's still on the court. The whole exercise was more cathartic than cabalistic."

She stared at me, a blank look on her face.

"That means liberating," I said.

She snorted. "I know what cabalistic means."

This conversation needed to get back on track. Not only would Boise be good repeat business, but she was a hot commodity. Word would get around. The clients would return. If they didn't, by the end of the month I'd be living out of my Prius.

"A good witch is part life-coach, part therapist," I said.

"I already have a life-coach *and* a therapist." She put down her coffee and jabbed a finger at me. "What I don't have, but what I need, is a witch who can put the whammy on Jason Sugarman, so I can get my movie career out of first gear."

"I can't just wiggle my nose." I smiled sheepishly. "Let's work on creating a positive energy field around you. I have these marvelous scented candles handcrafted by Bhutan monks. They're made of the wax from Asian pears grown in the Chele Le Grove. That's a virgin forest where no machinery of any type is permitted. Light the candles before you go to sleep and repeat a mantra that I'll give you. I guarantee your aura will be a deep blue in no time."

Boise stood. "This is ridiculous." She pulled out her phone. "Refused to take my concerns seriously."

"What are you doing?"

"I'm one-starring you on Yelp. Office décor embarrassingly outdated. And the coffee is weak." She tapped away as she walked out the door.

***

I struck the punching bag with a blazing left-right-left combination, followed up with an elbow, then a knee strike. I reset and kicked the bag with my bare right foot.

Kicking isn't a completely accurate description. In Pradal Serey, you don't snap your leg. Instead you generate power by rotating your hips, thus delivering maximum force against your target. And it firms up your glutes. I continued to imagine Boise as the bag, pummeling her with all my rage.

"Someone's fired up," said Daevy Sayavong, my kick-boxing coach. She's five-three, two inches shorter than me, but all muscle beneath her Dodgers t-shirt and shorts. Her mop of jet-black hair and intense eyes contrasted with her eternally goofy grin.

Gasping, I asked, "Why would you say that?" Left. Right. Right elbow. Left elbow. Right knee strike. Left kick. Left knee strike. Right kick.

"Take a minute, catch your breath, and grab a drink. Then I'll let you have a go at me."

I nodded, retreated from the bag, and sat. While sweat dripped down my forehead and stung my eyes, I chugged an organic, non-GMO electrolyte, swapped out my bag gloves for sparring gloves, and slipped the chest protector over my tank top.

The gym was empty except for Daevy and me. Checkerboard-style black and gray pads covered the floor. Exercise equipment crowded along the far wall. Above me hung the flag of Cambodia: two blue stripes and one red with Angkor Wat in the center.

The icepick-sharp keyboard stabs of Duran Duran's "A View to A Kill" blared from the sound system. A ten-year-old Daevy escaped the killing fields by walking all the way to Thailand. She came to

America as a refugee in the mid 80s and fell shamelessly in love with New Wave bands.

I met Daevy in the center of the gym. We touched gloves and began to spar. Daevy's a pro. No way I can keep up with her. Normally she doesn't go full out. Her students don't learn much when they're flat on the mat. But today, she wasn't holding back.

I successfully blocked a kick from the right, but before I could blink, she was on the other side of me, and dropped me with an elbow.

She offered a hand. "Are you going to tell me what's bothering you?"

"Nope," I mumbled through my mouth guard, getting to my feet. I launched right-left-right, elbow, and knee strike. She stopped them all.

Synthesizers and saxophones soared. "Gold" by Spandau Ballet was playing now.

I blocked a flurry of punches, but a quick knee felled me.

She stood over me. "Someone's not focused."

I was breathing too heavily to answer. Three more knockdowns and fifteen minutes later we're sitting on the bench.

"You're not here today, Jen." She tapped the side of her head.

I frowned. "It's business. Lost another client." I told her about Boise.

Daevy shrugged and pointed to my heart. "The wisest person I know once told me that success is all in here."

"If I'm the wisest person you know, then you've got bigger problems than me."

"Some air-headed reality-star trying to extend her fifteen minutes doesn't want to hire you? You're better off without her." She put her hand on my shoulder. "Remember Jim with his PTSD? You help real people with real problems."

I appreciated Daevy's efforts, but her pep talk wasn't going to pay the rent. I hit the shower, let the water flow over my aching muscles, and tried to forget about everything. It worked until the hot water ran out.

I stepped out of the shower, dried off, got dressed, and pulled my hair back into a ponytail. I found Daevy in the gym. Her smile was missing, replaced by a look of concern.

"You've got a potential client waiting," she said.

"Here?"

Daevy nodded. "Yeah. Says he went to your home, but got no answer. But Mrs. Beanpole noticed him and said where to find you. He's outside. If you want, I can run him off."

"Why? Are you getting a bad vibe from him?"

Daevy shook her head. "Not bad, just odd."

"I'm not in a position to turn down clients. Why don't you come out with me? If things get crazy, it'll be two against one." Not that Daevy needed any help to take down weirdoes.

We stepped outside into the midday sun, and I spotted him leaning against a mailbox. Daevy was right. This guy looked off. He was dressed like an extra from the latest unnecessary *Robin Hood* remake: a green vest over a white shirt, green tights, a triangular felt hat, and a leather punch looped over his shoulder. Plus, he wore a cape!

He saw us standing at the gym entrance, straightened up, and strode toward us with a definite sense of purpose. He stopped three feet before me, removed his hat, dropped to one knee, and bowed.

I glanced at Daevy who rolled her eyes.

In an accent I couldn't quite place, the man in green said, "Well met, Jennifer Griffiths, The Witch of Sherman Oaks. I am Braxtiaran Darahenij and I urgently need your assistance."

***

Ten minutes later, I was sipping my unsweetened iced tea in the far corner booth of the Boulevard Café. Brax (no way I was trying to pronounce his full name) ordered a milk and wasn't too pleased.

"This beverage is the product of unhappy bovines herded into exceedingly confined circumstances." He slammed the glass to the table. "It has been scorched, subjected to some malevolent mechanical process, and denuded of its essential nutrients. It is unworthy of being drunk."

Brax had dirty blonde hair, an infectious smile, and a strong chin. I was still trying to place his accent. New Zealand?

"Yeah, I do hate denuded milk." I fake-frowned in mock sympathy. "You said you needed my assistance?"

"Yes!" He held up a smartphone. "This ingenious device allowed me to peruse the ratings of witches and others imbued with the supernatural in the vicinity. You have received many outstanding testimonials. Save for this most recent assessment: 'Refused to turn the bastard who's ruining my career into a frog.'" His blue eyes, the color of Big Bear Lake, twinkled. "You are not only a lady of immense power and rare beauty, but of great integrity."

My face burned red. "I hope you're not looking for help with a casting call."

He gave me a bewildered look. "No, I require your aid in defeating the Evil Sorcerer Crixon."

"Evil Sorcerer Crixon?" I sighed.

He nodded. "The Spiteful One's followers plan to breach the dimensional barrier that protects your planet. They will open the portal allowing Crixon to manifest himself in all his malevolence."

I nodded politely and sipped my tea.

"I know what you're thinking," Brax said.

"Really?" *Why didn't I ask Daevy to come along? How am I going to get out of here? What asylum did you escape from?*

"Why not prevent the portal from opening, thus stopping the Sorcerer before he even arrives?" Brax shook his head. "The threat would never be truly gone, for the portal could open at any time. Crixon must be defeated here. Once that is done, the barrier cannot be breached for another 144,000 years." He paused. "That's Thacriulean years, of course."

"Of course." Time to make a break for it. I gulped the rest of my tea and stood. "Look, Brax. This all seems very interesting, but I have to go, I'm exp—"

"But you can't leave yet. We haven't even discussed your payment."

"Payment?" I returned to my seat.

He reached into his pouch and pulled out a fist of gold coins. They rattled on the table. "Will this be sufficient recompense?"

My eyes widened. I picked up one of the coins. Heavy. A Krugerrand? Was Brax's accent South African?

"The portal will open in your Mojave Desert. All the dedicated servants of Crixon: the duskmouths, the gallcrackles, and Dadan Sanguis, his high priestess, will be present at the ceremony."

"The desert? You mean like Burning Man?"

Brax nodded. "There will be a figure aflame. That is a necessary prerequisite for the portal to materialize."

Now it all made sense. Brax was larping one of the Merry Men because he's some kind of Renaissance Fair performer. And he needed me to fill a role. "Is this a union gig? Because I'm no longer in Actor's Equity."

"No guild membership is required to oppose the sorcerer."

I rubbed the coin between my fingers. I needed to make sure this was really gold, but this might be the break I'd been waiting for. "What exactly do you need me to do?"

"I would never presume to tell a witch how to use her powers."

His act was beginning to wear. "I'm not asking how, but what?"

"You stand upon the greensward, challenge the Sorcerer, and use your magic to defeat him. Once vanquished he will return to his home dimension and the portal will close."

"Where in the desert?

"The closest populace is a village called Baker."

I knew it. Off I-15. Little place to grab gas and snacks on the way to Vegas. "When is this?"

"The ceremony begins an hour before sundown."

"Today?"

"Yes, time is of the essence."

I gathered up the coins and slipped them into my purse. "I sure don't want to disappoint the duskcrackles and gallmouths, but we'll have to make a couple of stops first."

***

"I have no idea who this is." My buddy Arman, the proprietor of 24-7 Pawn, held the gold coin in his stubby fingers and displayed the profile of a lady in a crown. "Or what the hell this is." He flipped the coin over. The reverse featured some kind of half-beaver, half-dinosaur creature. "No numismatic value whatsoever."

"But it is gold, right?" I asked.

"Yeah, the tests say it's gold." He glanced at the stack of coins on the counter. "Where'd you even get these, anyway?"

Brax, further down the counter and fascinated with an over-sized metronome, answered, "They come direct from the Pagash Treasury, a reward from my good friend, the Countess Battenstrong."

Arman raised a bushy eyebrow. "The Countess Battenstrong?"

"I'm sure it's totally legit." I gathered up the coins. "Let's finish up in back."

I left Brax to the metronome, while Arman and I worked out a deal. I convinced him to trade the gold for cash, enough to pay off all my credit cards, rent an office that wasn't attached to my kitchen, and think about a vacation. Arman agreed not to report the transaction. I'm a good liberal and think everyone should pay their taxes, especially the multinationals that run this country. But does the government need more from me? What are they going to do with it? Drone strike another wedding party in Yemen?

Next stop: my place. I changed into my favorite turquoise golf shirt, dressy khaki shorts, and these fabulous ankle boots I discovered in a little boutique in West Hollywood. Black leather with a silver buckle and a two-inch heel. No time to go hit the salon. I wore my hair up, secured with a copper jaw-clip.

I called my friend Laura and let her know about this latest gig and had her track my iPhone. Into my purse I slipped three bottles of water and a five-shot .38 caliber revolver. Belonged to my granddad. I knew martial arts, but Brax, as charming and goofy as he was, had height, weight, and reach on me. The gun made for a great equalizer, just in case.

Three hours later, we were in my Prius heading north on 127 out of Baker toward Death Valley. The sun low in the western sky. The GPS instructed me to turn right onto a dirt road cutting across the desert.

"Is this really the way?" I asked.

"Indeed. Follow this path and we will arrive at the site of Venomous One's materialization." Brax annoyingly refused to break character.

The road was bumpy but survivable by keeping the speed under ten mph. We drove past miles of still landscape: brown rocks, Joshua trees, and sand, but not a single living creature. After thirty minutes or so, the road twisted around a mountain. Flames became visible in the distance.

Brax muttered something in a foreign language, then said, "Stop here."

I pointed to the GPS. "We still have a mile to go."

He shook his head. "We will approach on foot."

I pulled off the 'road', parked on a flat spot, and checked my phone: no bars. I stepped out of the air-conditioned car into the blazing heat. The desert wind sucked the moisture right out of me.

We walked toward the fire, Brax leading the way. I chugged half a bottle of water and offered the rest to Brax. He declined.

"Aren't you hot in that getup?" I asked.

"We have far greater concerns than my comfort."

No sound, but the wind and the crunch of our footsteps. As we grew closer, I could see the burning figure was neither a man nor boy. It had multiple tentacles, like a giant flaming squid. Had to be fifty feet tall. The wind died down. A low noise in the distance. Not shouting or chanting, not even sure it was voices. More like growling.

Ten minutes later we're at the camp, for lack of a better word. Decidedly low-tech. No ticket takers, info booth, or porta-potties. I couldn't even see where everyone parked.

The giant burning squid overlooked a green circle maybe one hundred feet in diameter. A giant putting green incongruously placed in the middle of the desert.

Brax led me to a large boulder where we perched ourselves to gain an unobstructed view of the ceremony.

Scores of cosplayers sat at edge of the circle. Most were wearing gray rubber, full-body suits, complete with pointed ears and tusks. Brax said those were the duskmouths. Not sure how they managed to sit down with their knees bending the wrong way. One grabbed a passing scorpion, and it looked like he shoved it in his mouth. Must be the heat getting to me. I drank more water.

Brax pointed out the gallcrackles: orange, bald, and equipped with a pair of realistic-looking prosthetic arms. The arms appeared to be functional, as one of the gallcrackles used all four to toss wood at the base of the flaming squid. Inside that guy must be sweating up a storm. Got to give them credit; these people were serious about putting on their show.

I chugged my last bottle of water. I hopped up and walked over to the closest duskmouth. I scrunched up my nose at the odor from his costume. Like a skunk drowning in burning motor oil. "Hey, do you have anything to drink?"

He gurgled at me unintelligibly.

"I appreciate your commitment to the role, but I'm parched. I need something before I do the big act."

He emitted a high-pitched wail and blue smoke emerged from his nostrils and ears.

"Wow that's some good effect," I muttered to myself as I walked back to Brax. "I need some water."

"Not now." He pointed to the circle. "The high priestess Dadan Sanguis is about to open the portal."

The priestess was the only one not wearing a rubber-suit. She was tall, about six feet, and built like a WWE Diva. She had platinum blond spiky hair and wore a strapless black gown that defied gravity. Don't tell me she didn't have work done. On either side of her, gallcrackles, using all four arms, pounded on drums. Da-dum, ba-dum, ba-thum.

The priestess chanted, danced, pointed her arms at the heavens, and chanted some more.

I leaned over to Brax. "When are we going to get to the good stuff?"

"Shh! He arrives."

Above the priestess a black hole appeared. I glanced around for projectors, but didn't see any. Then, an explosion. Gray smoke filled the air, when the smoke cleared, a man stood in the center of the green circle: The Evil Sorcerer Crixon.

Of course, he didn't come through the black hole. Good illusion. But the smoke was a dead giveaway. A chance to distract the audience. I should know. For three years, I was the assistant to the Astounding Melvin at Harrah's Lake Tahoe. Two shows daily. Dark on Mondays. *The Reno Gazette-Journal* named us a "Top Ten Entertainment Value of 2014."

Crixon strutted around the putting green waving a wand. He was an inch or two shorter than the priestess. Salt-and-pepper hair ran down to his shoulders. He wore something resembling a purple tuxedo. The smirk on his face reminded me of a certain Supreme Court Justice.

"Prepare yourself, Jennifer. It is nearly your time." Brax put a hand on my shoulder. "Crixon will announce the challenge. It's mandatory and perfunctory. No one is expected to accept. But you will. Say these words: *Hyvaksin teedan hausteesy.*

Then enter the greensward, where you will use your magic to defeat him and return him to Thacriulea. His minions will follow and the portal will close."

"After I accept the challenge, what do I say?"

Brax gave me a baffled look. "You are the witch. You know what spells are best."

"Ah, improvise." I nodded. "How long should it take? I want to give the audience their money's worth. They probably don't want me to dispatch Crixon in two minutes."

For the first time there was concern in his eyes. "Do not underestimate The Odious One. He has slashed a course of death and destruction across a dozen dimensions. I have confidence that you can defeat him and protect your world, but do not take your task lightly."

The drums stopped. No noise but the howling wind. Crixon glanced around the circle at his followers. He shouted in a language I didn't understand.

"Your turn," said Brax.

"Get some good photos of me. Something Instagramable." I handed him my purse and strode forward.

I stopped at the edge of the putting green. I announced in my most confident voice, *"Hivacstyn treidlen histeersi."*

Silence.

Crixon, the priestess, the minions all stared at me.

I realized I flubbed my lines and gave it another go. *"Havivacstine treeding hosteersi."*

Crixon glared at me, and the duskmouths made a sound like laughter. I turned back to get help from Brax, but he was already beside me.

In a booming voice Brax said, *"Hyvaksin teedan hausteesy."*

Crixon nodded.

"Sorry, I didn't get that right." I whispered to Brax. "What now?"

"The challenge has been accepted. Enter the greensward."

I stepped into the circle. "Welcome to California."

A look of amusement crossed Crixon's face. "Ah, a Terran. Who are you who dares to challenge me?" He had a British accent like one of the upper crusters on *Downton Abbey.*

I walked forward, trying not to trip as my heels sunk into the green, stopped about ten feet in front of him, and placed my hands on my hips. "I am Jennifer Griffiths, The Witch of Sherman Oaks, Defender of the Mojave, and Face of the New Resistance." I'd been rehearsing that line for hours.

The gallcrackles grunted.

Crixon looked me over and scoffed. "I sense no magic in you, Mortal. Leave now and spend your final few hours with your loved ones before I burn your world to a cinder."

"Not quite, Mister." I pirouetted on my left foot, spun three hundred and sixty degrees, pointed at him with my right hand. *"Esgusodwch fi, syr. Faint o arian y byddai'n ei gostio i gylchdroi teiars fy nghar!?"* It sounded impressive, but it was just Welsh for 'How much would it cost to get my tires rotated?'

For what I was getting paid, the audience deserved something more than 'Abra Cadabra.'

Crixon crossed his arms. "Is there more?"

I leaned forward, smiled, and said, *sotto voce* "Brax didn't give me a lot to go on. Say something and I'll react." I winked and stepped back.

Crixon raised his wand, and it sparkled with electricity. His eyes turned a flaming red. How he managed that trick, I had no idea. He uttered something unintelligible and pointed the wand at me. A lightning bolt streaked across the green, slammed into me, and knocked me backward through air. I thudded to the ground. Darkness swallowed me up.

*****

I opened my eyes. The light was dim, almost total darkness. My body ached all over. I tried to move my leg, but something held it in place.

"Jennifer, you are awake?" Brax asked.

I squinted. A manacle attached to my right shin, the chain secured to the wall. We were in what looked like a cave. "What the hell happened?" I licked dried blood from my lower lip. I needed water. My stomach on fire. My shirt was singed where the lightning bolt struck me, first-degree burns underneath. Damn. I really liked this shirt.

"Indeed, it is Hell. I was wrong." Brax shook his head. "I thought you were powerful enough to stop Crixon. I read how you placed a curse on one of your nation's greatest law-givers. You have a 4.9 rating on Yelp!"

"Enough with the act. Where are we?"

"Crixon's minions transported us to this abandoned mine. It is not far from the portal."

"This isn't funny anymore." Did Brax lead me into some kind of 21st century Manson Family sacrifice? "Get me out of this thing." I rattled the chain attached to my leg.

"Fair Witch, I cannot as I am similarly shackled. I have attempted to extricate myself with this." He held up a rusty crowbar. "So far, I have been unsuccessful."

"Knock it off with the cosplay. These people are nuts and dangerous. We have to get out of here and find help."

Brax frowned. "I doubt your secular authorities are any match for The Caustic One. That is why I sought you out. Perhaps I should have engaged the Oracle of Beverly Hills."

"Valerie? That hack? Everything she knows about being a witch, she learned from repeats of *Charmed*."

Brax opened his mouth, but didn't say anything.

I needed to focus. Losing my temper wasn't going to get us out of here. "Sorry, Brax, that was uncalled for." I took three deep breaths. "What's the deal with these people?"

"Deal?"

"What are they doing? Why are we chained up?"

"Crixon is going to sacrifice you to duskmouths. As for me, he will replace my soul with dark magic and I will become a drone in his army of destruction. The very same army that he will use to conquer and enslave your world." He sighed, his face covered with resignation.

It all seemed so impossible. But the gallcrackles? The portal? The lightning from Crixon's wand? I touched the burns on my stomach. Ow! That sure felt real.

Did I fail to block a strike from Daevy, and I'm KO'd on the floor of her gym, dreaming this? Or could it be another acid flashback? In either case, it doesn't matter what I do. Ride it out until I wake up or come down. But if Brax were right, the world was in danger.

First thing to do was to get out of these chains. Fortunately, whoever, or whatever, locked me up only secured one leg. My hands were free.

I removed my jaw-clip and my hair tumbled down. I bent the clip back-and-forth, weakening it until it snapped in half. The spring dropped into my palm and I inserted it into the manacle's lock.

"What are you doing?" asked Brax.

"My kind of magic." In one of our best illusions, The Amazing Melvin would handcuff me, stuff me in a burlap sack, and drop me into a giant aquarium. Picking this lock with two free hands while dry wasn't a challenge. In less than thirty seconds the lock popped open. I removed the manacle, stood, and stretched.

Brax's lock proved no more difficult. "Now we need to get out of here without being spotted and call for help."

Brax shook his head. "Your authorities are not armed with any weapons that can stop Crixon."

"He's never dealt with some of the good old boys they hire for Sheriff's deputies. They have hurting people down to an art," I said with false bravado. I wasn't sure how powerful Crixon was. I hoped Brax was overestimating him.

Brax stood. "We must confront him."

"He almost fricasseed me last time."

"Now you are prepared for him. If you were to use the element of surprise, we would defeat him effortlessly."

"No, Brax. I don't do that sort of magic. I do spirit guiding, affirmations, herbal workshops. Not lightning bolts."

"But I sensed great power in you."

"I think that was the Pradal Serey. I don't have a wand like Hermione."

He eyes lit up. "Can we contact this Hermione?"

"I think she's filming *Little Women*."

Brax gave me a blank look.

"We have to go. Are there any guards?" I asked.

"I do not believe Crixon posted any. They are not concerned with us, and the duskmouths do not want to miss any portion of the ceremony."

"OK, here's what we're going to. We're going sneak out of this mine as quietly as possible, head back to the Prius, and get the hell out of here. Once we're in cell range, I'm calling in the Highway Patrol, Homeland Security, and the Marines. They'll handle Crixon." I hope I sounded confident, because my knees were shaking.

"But, d—"

"No. We tried things your way, and I almost got bar-b-cued."

"I was going to say: Does not your transportation convenience require a key to start?"

My keys! "Where's my purse?"

Brax frowned. "It must have slipped from my grasp when the gallcrackles assaulted me."

No keys. Could I hotwire the Prius? Probably, given enough time, which I wasn't sure we had. But even if I were successful, I had no idea how to bypass the ignition interlock system.

Walk through the desert? It had to be at least twenty miles to the highway. Assuming we even went in the correct direction. And I was already dehydrated. The heat would probably get us long before we found the road.

I scowled. Chancing a repeat engagement with Crixon, lightning bolts, and his monsters was a crappy plan, but the only one I had. "We have to go back and get my purse."

"If we return, then we must face Crixon."

"No. I explained already. I'm not a real witch. I can't take him on. We sneak in, get the keys, sneak out, and go for help."

Brax wasn't happy, but nodded his assent. He picked up the crowbar, and we scrambled out of the mine. The entrance was in the side of a mountain a couple hundred feet above the circle. We switch-backed our way down. The duskmouths' and gallcrackles' attention was focused on the ceremony. Crixon gallivanted around the putting green using his wand to throw bolts of lightning and streams of flame. I touched my stomach where I was struck by the bolt and shuddered.

We reached the desert floor and slithered along the ground like snakes, not more than twenty feet from the circle, but no one took notice of us.

"Duskmouths are noted neither for intelligence nor ambition," Brax whispered.

We crawled our way to the boulder where we'd sat. The high priestess assembled ten duskmouths and stacked them in a pyramid. Crixon pointed his wand. An orange beam emerged from the wand and engulfed the pyramid of duskmouths with a brilliant flash. When the light returned to normal, a twelve-foot tall giant duskmouth stood where the pyramid had been. It would take a bazooka to bring that thing down. His little cousins squealed their approval.

I slipped behind the boulder and found my purse. Keys were inside. I looped the strap over my neck and slowly slunk back out. This might work after all.

"Okay, let's get out of here." I looked around but couldn't find Brax.

"Die, Repugnant One!" Brax charged across the circle, swinging the crowbar.

Crixon thrust the wand at him. A bolt struck Brax, knocking him to the ground.

"Brax!" I instinctively stood and raced toward him.

Crixon spotted me. A bolt of electricity crackled over my head. I ducked and ended flat in the dirt. He waved the wand, but instead of being struck by a lightning bolt, I floated into the air, drifting toward Crixon, my arms and legs pinwheeling to no effect. I landed in the circle, facing him.

"The so-called Witch of Sherman Oaks? It seems we'll have to revise the schedule and prepare your sacrifice now." There was that damned smirk again.

I tried not to shake. In the bravest voice I could muster, I said, "Yeah, well. If it's all the same to you, I'll just be going." I turned to walk away, but my feet didn't work. I stuck to the green like a fly to flypaper.

He addressed his followers. "What shall it be, my minions? Do you want to see me flay the skin from this arrogant Terran or would you prefer to watch her burn?"

The duskmouths moaned. The gallcrackles groaned.

Crixon laughed cruelly. "My followers have spoken. Flailing it shall be!"

I couldn't move my feet, but my hands were free. I pulled the gun from my purse. I'd never shot anything other than a target at the range, but I didn't hesitate. I aimed at Crixon's chest, cocked the hammer, and pull— Something was wrong. The trigger wouldn't move. No, not the trigger. My finger froze. It wasn't doubt or fear. My finger simply wouldn't respond.

Crixon gestured with his wand.

The gun was hot to my hand, searing, I dropped it. My hand red, beginning to blister.

The revolver rose from the ground and floated in front of Crixon. A twist of his wand and the gun broke itself down, its parts suspended in midair. He inspected the pieces. A look of understanding crossed his face. "Ah, what a lovely toy. The hammer strikes the primer, igniting a propellant of potassium carbonate and potassium sulfate, which drives the bullet down the barrel." Crixon mumbled something, and the gun reassembled.

I struggled to free myself. My feet lifted, but the soles and heels of my boots stuck to the green. I flailed like one of those advertising balloons outside a car dealership.

Crixon aimed the gun at the giant duskmouth and fired. The bullet ricocheted harmlessly off its body. It made some sort of high-pitched noise, like a giggle. Guess it tickled.

"You have no magic, and your science is for children. This world will be an easy conquest." Crixon tossed the gun aside. "Where were we? Oh yes, my servants demand that I flay you alive."

He whispered something, and the wand transformed into a blade. He sliced the palm of his left hand and blood dripped to the ground. He gazed at the sky and began an incantation. The duskmouths and gallcrackles chanted.

My shoes were stuck to the circle, not my feet. I reached down and unsnapped the buckles. I flexed my foot and lifted it an inch to be sure.

Crixon approached, weapon in one hand, his other dripping blood. I had to time this perfectly. He raised the blade, aiming for my chest. I lifted my right leg, got excellent hip rotation, slammed my foot into his ribcage, and sent him sprawling. Daevy would be so proud. The blade slipped from his hand and returned to the form of a wand.

The minions grunted their disapproval.

"Earth isn't the pushover you think it is." I delivered a knee strike to his head. Almost.

Crixon raised his hands, blocked my blow, and grabbed my shin. I was off-balance, standing on my left foot, while he held my right leg. He twisted my leg, pain shot up my spine, and I fell to the ground.

I scrambled to my feet. He did the same. We faced off. I feinted to the right, moved to his left, and smacked him with an elbow. I blocked his fist and hit him with a roundhouse right. I was faster and a better fighter, but it was like hitting a punching bag, only harder. His skin was like armor.

I fought with no mercy. This was for the world. This was for me. Left, right, left, he covered up, and I kept pounding. He crouched and leg-swiped me, dropping me to the ground. He crawled toward the wand. I grabbed his leg. He wasn't making any progress, but I couldn't pull him away. Stalemate.

He shouted, and the wand shakily rose from the green, floating toward his outstretched hand.

The crowbar soared through the air and struck Crixon's hand. He screamed, and the wand dropped to the ground.

Brax! I looked to him for help, but a gallcrackle wrestled him to the ground. The minions formed a circle on the green and surrounded us, but they looked to be letting Crixon and me battle it out without interference.

I stomped on Crixon's leg, let him go, and stood. I needed a weapon. The gun was proven worthless. I looked for the crowbar. A duskmouth was chewing on it like an over-sized Tootsie Roll. That left the wand. I scrambled past Crixon as he rose. I picked up the wand, faced him, and waved like I had seen him do.

Nothing.

Crixon chortled. "The wand is useless to you. It requires a lifetime of training to master."

With the wand in my left hand I advanced, I feinted with a right. He moved to block, and I did my best impression of a Mike Trout homerun swing, slamming the wand into his groin. No such thing as dirty fighting when the world is at stake. A wide-eyed Crixon whimpered and dropped to the ground. I pounded him in the head with the wand until he lapsed into unconscious, the smirk wiped off his face.

Exhausted I dropped to my knees and gulped deep breaths of air.

"Jennifer Griffiths, The Witch of Sherman Oaks, Defender of the Mojave, Face of the New Resistance." The voice of the high priestess came from directly behind me.

I was spent, nothing left, but the fight wasn't over. I gripped the wand with my left hand, balled my right into a fist. I counted to three and spun as I stood.

My knees collapsed. I tumbled to the ground; the wand slipped from my hand. The priestess stood over me. I held back my tears. I fought the good fight. I wasn't going out crying.

Dadan raised her hand. "You accepted Crixon's challenge and defeated him in fair combat. Mostly." Her eyes flicked to Brax. The gallcrackle released him and Brax was slowly picking himself up. "I declare you champion." She offered me her hand and lifted me to my feet. In a low voice she said, "I never liked working for that jerk."

The duskmouths broke into chant. "Henna-Thur! Henna-Thur!"

"Bunch of front runners," I muttered.

Brax addressed the priestess. "You will return to Thacriulea? Crixon, duskmouths, gallcrackles, all?"

Dadan nodded. She stamped her right foot twice, and the portal opened above us. "We will depart this world."

Crixon's unconscious body floated upward through the portal and disappeared. The giant duskmouth and the gallcrackles followed. The smaller duskmouths ascended. They twisted their heads to get a look at me while still doing their best to chant my name. The priestess was the last to go. The portal closed, and the green vanished. We stood on sand. In the west the sky was a dark purple.

I grabbed Brax and gave him a big hug. "It's over right? You said he can't come back."

"The portal cannot re-open for 144,000 years."

"So, what now?" I asked.

"Earth is safe. Return to your life."

"And what about you?"

"There is more evil that threatens other worlds. My work never ends."

"In that case, do me a favor. Next time you choose a defender, engage in a little more research."

Brax smiled. "Jennifer Griffiths, you are a true champion. I could not have selected any better."

I kissed him on the cheek. "If you're ever in Sherman Oaks again, look me up."

My gaze flicked to the revolver laying on the ground. "Don't want to forget this." I reached down. By the time I straightened up, Brax was gone.

The sun had completely set. The squid burned itself out. New moon. And as dazzling as a night sky full of stars is, it wasn't enough light to find my way to the Prius. I took half-a-dozen steps in what I hoped was the right direction and stubbed my toe on something metal. Half-buried in the sand, I found Crixon's wand.

I picked it up and gave it a wave. Still no lightning, flames, energy beams. But I'd hold on to it: a souvenir from the time I saved the world.

My black boots were impossible to find in the dark. So I trudged off barefoot in search of my car. An hour of tripping over cacti and rocks, left me no closer to locating the Prius. I sat on a boulder, laid the wand down, rubbed my scratched and swollen feet, and considered waiting until sunrise. I swallowed to get the saliva going in my mouth. Should have asked for water before everyone disappeared.

Frustrated I shouted at the desert, "Where's my damn car?"

The wand rattled and hummed. In the distance my Prius lit up, surrounded by a shower of blue neon light.

Perhaps the wand would be more than a souvenir.

***

We sat on the deck of my Manhattan Beach office. Cynthia, my new client, and I sipped lemonade in the shade, while watching the waves roll in.

Cynthia set down her glass. "My boss is impossible. He's making all sorts of creepy demands, and says if I don't go along, he'll have me fired." She lowered her voice like she was confiding a secret. "I was wondering if you could put some sort of curse on him."

My fingers stroked the cold hard metal of the wand. "What did you have in mind?"

THE END

The Last Mission

Across the street, three assailants in dark coats forced a smaller man into the alley. It had been ten years since I'd been in Ramoria, but the country was crime ridden as ever. I ignored sounds of a struggle. Those of us who want to enjoy our pensions one day know better than to get involved with the locals. Plus, I was due a briefing at the embassy in fifteen minutes. Don't want to be late and upset the desk jockeys.

"Help! Help!" cried a tiny voice somewhere to my left.

Sounded like the call of a child. The voice continued to plead for assistance. Training at The School taught us to focus on the mission and ignore other matters.

But this was a child in need.

The pleas led me to four men gathered around a rain barrel. Their clothes sagged on bony bodies. One wore a gray flat cap. All four smoked. The odor of cheap tobacco overpowered the city's rank combination of manure and garbage.

In the barrel a brown mouse splashed, struggling to stay afloat. The mouse cried; the men laughed. These cretins were torturing an intelligent animal! The mouse paddled to the edge of the barrel, only to have one of the men use a stick to push the mouse back to the center.

Forget rules, forget protocol.

"How much for the mouse?" I affected an upper-class Ramorian accent, consistent with my attire. "A talking creature would be a perfect surprise for my daughter. Today is her birthday."

"When bets are paid," said Gray Cap, "and if it survives the contest. Then we talk price."

The mouse flailed, not making any progress toward the edge. He swallowed a mouthful of water and could no longer shout.

"A dead pet isn't much of a present for a young girl," I said.

The men laughed.

I asked the one on my left, "How much did you wager?"

"Five soldos that the rodent drowns." He's eyes widened. "Yes, yes! He's going down!"

A pittance. Even if the others laid three times as much, two libras would more than cover the bets.

"I haven't time to wait. This is more than a fair price." I flipped two silver coins to Gray Cap and scooped up the mouse with my left hand. His fur was slippery, and he almost squirmed away.

The gamblers voiced their disapproval. The one who bet five soldos grabbed my left arm. In an instant, my dagger was out of its sheath and pressed against his neck.

Gray Cap said, "Dimitar, this gentleman is correct. It is a shame to deprive his daughter of such a wonderful gift. How old is she, sir?"

"Seven."

A trickle of blood ran down Dimitar's neck.

Gray Cap smiled, revealing several missing teeth. "Fellows, surely our game of amusement is nothing compared to the joy of a young girl on her seventh birthday."

Dimitar released my arm and backed away, while the others muttered their assent. I returned my blade to its place on my belt and left the gamblers to devise some new depravity.

The mouse stopped panting. He lay exhausted in my hand and shivered in the wind. I dried him with my handkerchief. With care, I deposited him in the breast pocket of my coat, where he curled in a ball and pressed against my chest.

Instead of continuing to the embassy, I walked east past the train station toward a row of shops. The odds that this mouse and those cretins were part of an operation were astronomical. But that's the same thinking that allowed Bandar Station to place a beagle in the home of Valoran Army Chief of Staff. The intelligence that pup passed along shortened the war by six months.

Squeezed between a butcher and a barber, I found a small general store. Inside, the paint was peeling and the floorboards uneven. Various wares combined to produce an eye-watering aroma worse than the city itself. The proprietress, a scowling woman with patchy white hair, overcharged me for a purported slab of fuzzy white rind. I tried a bit and made a face. The taste and consistency were like damp mud. I retrieved the mouse from my pocket and offered him a bite, hoping that mice have less discerning palettes.

His nose twitched. "Thank you, but I rather don't care for cheese," he said in a high-pitched squeak.

"A mouse who doesn't like cheese?"

"It's an enduring myth, sir. But most mice don't like cheese. It gives us terrible indigestion."

"Then what would you prefer?" I asked.

"A bit of pear. Or any fruit, really."

I rummaged through bins of rotten fruit. No pears. The best piece was a sickly green apple blemished on one side. I carved a slice. Dry and sour.

"I'm afraid it's not that good." I cut the mouse a smaller slice.

"The elders of my nest tell tales of when fruit was plentiful and sweet. The drought's been tough on the farms and orchards." He nibbled. "Not the worst I've tasted."

"What you got there?" The shopkeeper emerged from behind the counter.

"This is..." I faced the mouse. "I'm afraid I don't know your name."

"I am Basilius." He bowed.

"This is my new acquaintance, Basilius." I held him out in my palm.

"Take it out." She pointed to the door. "I don't allow that kind in my store."

"We shall leave, but first allow me to say that for a cheese," I held up the slab, "you've produced a first-rate emetic."

She shook her fist. "Out! Or I call the constable."

Back on the street the sun had broken through the clouds and the wind died down. Basilius scampered halfway up my sleeve, leapt into my outer coat pocket, then poked his head out. "I'd be a very inconsiderate mouse if I didn't thank you, Mister..."

"John Linn, at your service."

"Mr. Linn, thank you for your intervention and your generosity. I think that I shall make a wonderful pet for your daughter."

It wasn't my daughter's birthday. She didn't exist. And taking him into the embassy was out of the question. "Wouldn't you prefer to be free and return to your own nest?"

He squeaked. "But I am in your debt. I take such matters seriously."

"As do I." This mouse was more honorable than most humans. "When the time comes, your nest or your nest's pups may repay me."

"Mr. Linn, I will tell my brothers and sisters of your benevolence, and we shall fulfill our obligation to you."

I cut another slice from the apple for Basilius and handed it to him as I picked him from my pocket. He jumped from my hand without waiting to be lowered to the ground, tumbling to the street with the chunk of apple in his paws. Still holding the slice, the brown mouse disappeared into a crack between two stores.

***

A roundabout fifteen-minute walk to ensure I wasn't followed delivered me to our embassy. The four-story alabaster building dwarfed its neighbors. A six-foot iron fence topped with spikes surrounded the grounds. The embassy once belonged to one of the city's wealthier merchants. When the Granite Revolution arrived, his success left the merchant a marked man, earning him a trip to the wall.

At the gate, a couple of MSCs in their magenta dress uniforms stood at attention. Despite my Ramorian garb, I didn't rate a glance. The embassy was open for business and all manner of people were coming and going.

Inside, expensive art lined the walls and fancy sculpture filled the halls. The Foreign Ministry's decorating budget appeared to have escaped the Assembly's spending cuts. I announced myself to a bored-looking clerk and took a seat.

A couple of minutes later, a young woman with brown hair and eager eyes appeared. "Mr. Linn?"

I stood and offered my hand.

"Margaret Mehan, with the Foreign Service," she said, not offering her own. "You're late."

My hand still extended, I didn't reply.

"Follow me."

On second glance, she wasn't just young, but practically a kid. Twenty-three or four, tops. "Been assigned to the embassy for long?" I asked.

She led me to the cube which was buried two stories down in the sub-basement and past the furnace. Iron walls, floor and ceiling. Impervious to supernatural eavesdropping. Inside three chairs and a table covered with folders and maps. A man in an ill-fitting suit studied them. This was not Bryan Miller.

She cleared her throat. "Major Rowe? John Linn is here."

He looked up from the table. "So, you're Linn, eh?"

Mehan grabbed the metal knob and swung the door shut.

I waited for the clanging echoes to subside. "Yes."

"You're late." Rowe was my age, or maybe a bit older. Salt-and-pepper hair. Must have put on twenty pounds since he bought that suit.

"Have a chair," said Rowe. He and Mehan took seats on the opposite side of the table.

I sat. "What happened to Miller?"

Rowe squinted at me. "I'm running this op, Linn. Miller's back at The Hill. Been gone close to a month."

"How come?"

"Administrative matter," said Mehan. "That's all we're permitted to say."

I didn't like that. Miller was one of the best in Ops Planning. Without proper preparation, you can blow a mission before it even starts. I had no desire to rot in a Ramorian military prison because someone didn't do his (or her) homework.

"Are you permitted to say how long you've been at the embassy?" I asked Mehan.

"I wasn't being rude." Mehan sighed. "I was maintaining security by not discussing matters outside the cube."

"That's not an answer," I said.

"I've been in-country for six weeks. But I wrote my senior thesis on the origins and causes of the

Granite Revolution. I'm well acquainted with both recent history and the current state of affairs in Ramoria."

Great. A toddler who thinks she knows it all.

"Let's move on." Rowe tapped a folder. "Good service record, Linn. I was at the Battle of Morgan's Pass, too. Forty-Fifth Sappers. Hell of a party."

Morgan's Pass. A pointless battle in a war fought because two princes fell in love with the same mermaid. Our brilliant general leading us into an ambush. Half my squad dying on a no-name hill, the snow red with blood.

"Yeah. It was cold," I said.

He roared. "Thought I'd freeze my ass off." He put my file down, picked up a new folder and opened it. "Here's the deal. The Hill needs to know the location of the Ramorian Second Fleet and if they've added any new ships."

I nodded.

"Naval Base at Corvis Bay is your assignment." He pointed to the map and circled the location with a black marker.

"Location, size and composition? Simple recon. Why not use seers?" I said.

"We have," said Mehan. "Can't get a read. They see nothing but gray."

Rowe grunted. "Never thought those non-coms were reliable. We had a privateer off the coast launch albatrosses and condors to take a look. None returned."

"So, eyes on the ground," I said.

"Exactly." Rowe pointed at the map. "The fleet could be elsewhere. Corvis Bay is our best guess. Could be at the mouth of the Fytyer River, docked at Mannen Shipyards or conducting exercises at sea. We've got agents checking those possibilities. But we need to know. Now."

"Why? What's up?" I said.

"That's classified," said Mehan. "All I can say is relations with Ramoria are on a knife's edge."

Were we close to war? Mehan's face betrayed no secrets.

"You'll take the train from Lavko to Mejica. Margaret's made a reservation for you at a rooming house across from the station." Rowe made another mark on the map. "From there it's a short carriage ride, or a long walk, to these hills. Hike to the top and you'll have a perfect view of the bay."

I frowned. "I'm just supposed to go traipsing around the countryside near a Ramorian Naval Base?" God, I missed Miller.

"It's mostly nature preserves," said Mehan. "An excellent area for bird-watching."

"My cover is I'm a birdwatcher?" Instead of wasting away in a cell, I had visions of a firing squad.

Mehan handed me a folder. "You're Professor Michael McCarthy, ornithologist from Western Aslamia University. You're hiking in the hills surrounding Corvis Bay, cataloguing indigenous avians for your newest publication."

I looked over the bio on McCarthy: thirty-six, never served, unmarried. Quite the raconteur and ladies' man. An attached photo showed a handsome man with perfect teeth. I understood his romantic success.

"And the real Professor McCarthy?" I said.

"The professor is away and unreachable," said Mehan. "At a secluded beach house carrying on a torrid affair with the wife of a colleague. Any inquiries at the University will confirm he, or rather you, are in Ramoria on expedition."

"Once you've seen whether the fleet is in port, send a telegram to the embassy." Rowe handed me a sheet. "Memorize this code."

Colors for numbers: White for one, brown for two, etc. Birds for ships: Hawks are cruisers, sparrows are frigates, woodpeckers are ships of the line. No ships in the bay, work the word 'devoid' into the message. Amateur stuff. This mission looked worse by the minute.

But if war was in the offing, as I was beginning to suspect, I'd stand-up straight, salute, and follow orders. There was no way I would let a bunch of mothers lose their sons, because I didn't take these amateurs and their mission seriously.

"As soon as we locate the fleet, our other agents will be recalled," said Rowe. "These documents can't leave the cube. But you can take the trail maps and this." He handed me a hefty book.

Migratory Birds of the Eastern Hemisphere by Dr. Michael M. McCarthy. At least someone in Documents was on the job. The dust jacket featured my smiling mug.

***

A throng of foul-smelling beggars, peddlers, and assorted vagrants filled the main concourse of Lavko's Central Station. Stepping over and around the rabble, I took pity on a blind beggar and tossed a soldo in his bowl. At the sound of the clanking coin, he thanked me.

My generosity was a mistake, marking me as an easy touch. Tramps clawed at my legs. A man in a threadbare Ramorian Army coat, but no shoes rose to block my path.

"Help a veteran out, sir?" He held out his hand.

I passed by without comment. He grabbed my arm. I spun and elbowed him in the chest. He staggered backward and fell upon two beggars. The horde howled their disapproval, but made no more attempts to obstruct me.

I checked my watch. Thirty minutes before the train departed. I found relief from the masses inside a tiny café off the main concourse. I ordered two biscuits and coffee. The biscuits were stale, the jam watery, the butter flavorless. I took the map of the nature preserve from my knapsack and studied it while I sipped the bitter coffee and ate half a biscuit.

"Read your fortune, sir? Learn the future about your love and life," a female voice said.

No respite, even in the cafe. I looked up from my map. The woman was pretending to be a soothsayer. She wore the requisite green robe. Her silver hair flowed past her shoulders. I was most impressed by her purple eyes. Most fakers didn't go to the trouble of coloring their irises.

I waved her away. "I've done well enough on my own."

"Have you, Randolph?"

Randolph.

Somewhere buried deep in the bowels of War Department's archives, my enlistment papers revealed my real name. But no one within a thousand versts of here could know it. Either that was the luckiest wild guess, or she was the real deal. "Okay," I said. "What's my future?"

She held up a pair of fingers. "Two soldos."

"I don't suppose I can get a receipt for this." I handed her the coins. "I'm on an expense account."

She grabbed the coins. "And something to eat."

"Here." I shoved the plate toward her. "Have mine."

She grabbed the half-eaten biscuit and shoveled it into her mouth.

I gave her time to chew. "Now, about my future."

"Give me your hand."

I offered my left hand. She clasped it between hers. Her body shook, head tilted backward, eyes rolled upward, leaving white orbs. If she weren't real, she had the act down pat.

"Randolph," she said in a ghostly voice.

"Let's skip the names."

"I see violence. Blood. Death."

"I don't need to know my past. I lived it."

"A man with salt-and-pepper hair. He is not your friend."

Okay, she's not a faker. "Tell me something I don't know."

"Your journey is fraught with peril."

"For two soldos, I'm expecting specifics."

She clasped harder. "I see gray mist. Black water."

"Anything useful?"

"Cows. Many cows. The cows lead to freedom."

"Now you're just making stuff up." I extricated my hand from hers.

"You have been forewarned, Randolph. This will be your last mission."

"You were going to tell me about future love."

The purple irises rolled back into place. She grabbed the other biscuit, slathered it with tasteless butter and scampered away.

"That was certainly worth two soldos," I said to empty air.

***

Sleep eluded me on the train ride from Lavko to Mejica. The hard seats, noisy engine, and bumpy rails made any rest impossible. The landscape consisted of nothing more than lifeless brown fields. Didn't it ever rain in this country? The train stopped every couple of hours at smaller towns and once again on the outskirts of Mejica to load and unload livestock.

From what I could see, Ramoria didn't look ready for any kind of fight. The perpetual drought had left the populace malnourished and demoralized. Perhaps that's what our leaders were counting on: a weak enemy, easily defeated.

Mejica Station was little more than a ticket/telegraph office and a water tower. No room for a throng of vagrants to accost me. I crossed the street to the rooming house and turned in early.

The bed was adequate, and I enjoyed a decent night's sleep. Rising before daybreak, I futzed in the kitchen. Brown bread with honey and coffee for breakfast. I filled my thermos with more coffee, canteens with water, and slipped the bread into my knapsack.

Dressed for the trail, flannel shirt, khakis, hiking boots and cap to keep the sun off my head, I stepped out of the hotel into the pre-dawn darkness and felt the slightest tug at my pack. A dirty-faced boy of nine or ten held my wallet in his hand. I locked on to his arm with an iron grip.

"Sorry, sir. This was falling out of your pocket." He offered the wallet.

"Falling out of the zippered pocket of my bag?"

He shrugged. "Guess so."

"Perhaps we should see the constable about this."

"Don't do that, sir, I—"

He dropped the wallet. As I reached down to grab it, he stomped on my toe and twisted out of my grasp. He dashed away and disappeared into the pre-dawn darkness.

Perfect. I had no intention of speaking with the local authorities and raising my profile. The boy would think he was clever to escape from an old fool.

***

I headed out of Mejica on the West Shore Road. Four versts to the trailhead, according to my map. I figured I'd arrive about an hour after dawn. Five minutes later, a wagon approached from behind. For the price of a soldo, I convinced the farmer returning home after bringing his eggs and milk to give me a ride.

He deposited me without words at the trailhead. I squinted at the shabby sign marking the path. Binoculars around my neck and a notebook protruding from my shirt pocket, I looked quite the ornithologist.

To my right, the east, the sky was now a faint purple. Dawn at least thirty minutes away. I struck a match and re-checked my map. Confident of the way, I secured my pack and began the climb.

The trail was rocky, overgrown, and not much in use. At one point it disappeared into a boulder field. I scoured the other side, looking for the trail. The sun rose higher, and the sky became a dark turquoise. With the additional light, I picked up the trail and pushed forward.

In the second hour of my hike, a hawk circled overhead. Ramorian society's attitude toward talking animals made it likely he was a dumb predator, not a spy. I made dutiful notes in my journal and stopped every fifteen minutes to stare through my binoculars.

Three hours into my hike, the path grew steeper. I wasn't an eighteen-year-old recruit anymore. I stopped for rest, coffee, and to relieve myself in the bushes.

At four-plus hours, the blast of a shotgun exploded ahead on the trail. Another blast. I sang "Pete's Piece", an old tavern song popular with the enlisted. I wanted whoever was shooting to know I was headed in his direction. I was up to the fourth verse where Pete's best mate dies, when I rounded a thicket of trees and found two men on the trail.

Hunters. Both held shotguns, knapsacks on their back. One my age, the other younger. Both skinny. Had yet to see anyone overweight in this country.

"Good morning." I gave a friendly wave. They looked surprised to see me, or perhaps anyone. Must not have heard my singing.

The older man nodded. "I am Nikolai, this is my son Alexi." The son had a dull look to him.

"Michael." I nodded back.

"Usually don't see many on the trail. What brings you this way?" Nikolai asked.

I held up my binoculars. "Bird watching."

"You don't watch them. You eat them." Alexi laughed. "Shot a condor couple of weeks ago. Found it on the ground. Pleaded for its life." He mocked the voice. "Please..."

Nikolai smiled. "Clubbed its head in. Didn't taste any better than a dumb bird. Maybe worse."

These men were insufferably pleased with themselves for killing an intelligent being. Possibly one of our avians sent to observe the naval base.

The son had his shotgun uncocked and over his shoulder. The father's pointed to the ground. Hit the old man first. Sweep my legs and take him down. While he's down, advance on the son. An elbow to the throat crushing his larynx. He'd be no more trouble. Back to the old man. A blow to the head before he could stand again, while the son asphyxiated on the ground.

Forty seconds tops.

But I'd have to drag them off the trail. And bury the bodies. Two hours work at least, putting me behind schedule, plus the threat of more hunters or others stumbling across me.

Killing them would be satisfying, but if it led to the failure of the mission, the result could be thousands of deaths on both sides. So, I sat on a boulder making small talk with the father and forcing myself to laugh at the son's jokes. Drank some coffee. Ate some bread. Waved goodbye. Resumed my ascent.

The sun wasn't quite overheard when I passed the tree line. The trail petered out into a sea of rocks. Not physically difficult, but mentally taxing. Slowing my pace to avoid the wobbly stones, I gasped in the thin air. Two false summits fooled me. I checked my watch. The sixth hour of hiking.

The wind picked up. Must be near the summit now. I smiled. Rowe and Mehan's plan wasn't that awful. Catch my breath at the top, spy on the naval base through the binoculars, count the ships, and head back down. I figured I'd be back in town in time for an early dinner. As I crested the hill, my smile disappeared.

To the east, where Corvis Naval Base should be, was a blanket of gray fog.

***

Perhaps the seers weren't a bust. Could they have been unable to "see" the naval base because it was shrouded? Could fog last weeks or months?

I sat on a boulder drinking the last of my coffee, contemplating the view. To my left, the west, nothing but blue sky and ocean. Far below, white waves crashed against the shoreline. To my right, the east, impenetrable gray fog.

Instead of a cool and breezy summit, stifling hot air surrounded me. With no wind, the fog wasn't moving or breaking up.

A marmot, undernourished and with tufts of fur missing, scrambled over the rocks toward me. He halted a few feet away and looked up with hope in his eyes.

I broke off a crust of bread and tossed it to him. He gobbled it up in two seconds.

"Thank you," he said in a cracking voice.

"There's more if you can answer a few questions."

He advanced a few hesitant steps. "Ask."

"How long has the fog been here?"

The marmot shuddered. "Long time. Bad fog. Don't go in there."

"Don't go in the fog?"

The marmot nodded.

"Why not?"

"Fog is bad."

"Yeah, I got that. But why is it bad?"

"Fog is bad."

I shrugged. Didn't sound like I would get anything useful out of him. I tossed him another crust of bread and offered him a sip from my canteen. He guzzled half the container.

"You were thirsty."

"Yes. Fog is bad. No rain. No food. No water."

"Thanks for your help."

"Fog is bad," he repeated as he scampered away.

I re-checked the map. The trail switch-backed down to the bay. Descending the entire length wasn't an option. I couldn't risk encountering a Ramorian security patrol. With luck I'd find a gap in the fog before I crossed from the preserve onto the base.

Fifty steps down the trail, mountain on my right side, drop-off to the sea on the left, I stopped a foot short of the fog. Up close it looked more like mist, tiny particles floating immeasurably close together. The boundary between sunlight and gray was sharp, like a table's edge. Leaning forward, I puckered up and blew. The fog remained in place. I inserted my left arm into the gray mystery, wiggled my fingers, and found my hand obscured. Something on my skin, like crawling ants. I pulled my hand out of the fog, but there was nothing on it. When I pushed my hand back in, the feeling returned.

From my knapsack, I retrieved a mini-lantern, lit it and held it in the fog. Didn't help. I blew out the flame and packed away the lantern.

What was in the fog? What was the fog?

The Hill expected answers. Rowe and Mehan wanted a report. I hoped to avoid a war.

I took a deep breath, counted five and with one deliberate step entered the fog. The sun vanished. Nothing but gray on all sides. One stride down the trail was visible before the ground faded away. The air was hotter than at the summit with a faint aroma of lemons. The sensation of crawling ants covered my body.

One more step. Silence. No birds singing or waves crashing. Another step. My pace would be slow. Didn't want to go straight, where the trail zagged, and step off the mountain.

Though I was descending, my heart pounded. The heat grew more intense. Sweat soaked my clothes. Twenty minutes in I paused to stuff my hat in my knapsack, roll up my sleeves and mop my brow. The sensation of ants crawling on my skin persisted. Still no wind, but for the first time a buzzing noise, so faint I thought it was my imagination. I stood still; the sound seemed real.

Heights had never been a problem for me. Our unit scaled Gehring's Cliffs in the Five Weeks' War, while the enemy rained fire upon us. But the nagging fear of stumbling and falling off the side of the mountain found me grasping at rocks and scrubby bushes.

Forty minutes in and the gray had grown neither lighter nor darker. My hope for a break in the fog w—

Voices!

I plastered myself against the mountain and froze. Impossible to make out the words over the increasingly loud buzzing. The voices seemed to come from all around me.

My hands shook. I held my breath and strained my ears. No more voices. Five minutes. Still no voices. I waited five more, as sweat trickled down my back. Out of coffee, I retrieved a canteen and guzzled the water. The voices didn't return. Did I imagine them?

I resumed my descent at an even slower pace. At the next switchback my head spun; I imagined myself tumbling over the side. I dropped to a crouch, making the turn on my knees. My heart raced even faster. Did this fog ever end? I crawled down the trail, still sure I was going to slip over the side and plummet to my death. If I c—

More voices!

The tone and staccato of an officer issuing orders. I leaned against the rocks and discovered a crack in the side of the mountain. I squeezed my body into the darkness and crawled forward. To my surprise the crevice grew wider and became a cave.

I crawled in the dirt ten feet, twenty feet, thirty feet. My head bumped into rock. I sat on the ground, leaning against the cave wall, and lit my lantern. The roof was my height, and it was about twenty feet wide. A pile of animal bones laid in a long-discarded fire pit.

No more voices. The buzzing stopped. The ants stopped crawling. The only sound my own labored breathing. My hands trembled as I retrieved the canteen. It slipped from my grasp and dropped to the stone floor. The clattering echoed through the cave. Surely the patrol heard that. I froze again but couldn't hold my breath, on the verge of hyperventilating.

What the Hell was wrong with me? I'd been on more dangerous or stressful missions, but never reacted like this.

I closed my eyes. Focused on my training. Pushed the random thoughts from my mind. My shoulders drooped, chest slumped and the rest of my muscles fell limp. Counted backward from five hundred.

Calmness overcame me. My heart rate slowed. My breathing returned to normal. I grabbed the canteen.

The lemon taste of the fog was still in my mouth. Why did that seem familiar? A memory in the corner of my mind. Something about the odor of lemons. It wa—

A weird fog that was a meteorological impossibility? An old sergeant of mine told the story of a mist that smelled like lemons and drove men mad.

The Ramorians must have a tempestarius working for them. No, to hold the fog in place for months, meant multiple tempestarii. The extreme anxiety was a delightful bonus, designed to keep any spies or curious citizens from exploring. And the voices were a hallucination. They had to be. The drought wreaking havoc on the rest of the country was no doubt a side effect. To keep a military secret, the Ramorian government was ruining the harvest and starving their people.

Could Ramoria use the fog, or something like it, as a weapon? The prospect of war became even more worrying. I imagined the farms back home after months of no rain, the soil turning to dust and blowing away.

Not going any further. I'd wait until rested and the heat died down to retrace my steps to the summit. I closed my eyes, letting the calm wash over me. I rested, not asleep, but not quite awake. My mind a contented blank, until I was jolted into awareness by the smell of lemons.

I opened my eyes. Fog filled half the cave and was drifting in my direction. No wind on my face. Was it designed to seek intruders?

I wasn't thrilled with the idea of heading back out, but I'd lose my sanity trapped in here with that accursed fog.

Now that I knew my anxiety was supernaturally induced, I hoped logic and reason would be enough to guide me back to the summit. I packed away my mini-lantern, guzzled the last of my water and crawled through the mist and out of the cave. The buzzing in my ears returned, the taste of lemons strong in my mouth, ants marching all over me. I walked deliberately up the trail, favoring the side by the mountain. Kept my head down, focusing on every step.

The fear isn't real, it's only a spell. The fear isn't re—

Voices again!

I knew they had to be an effect of the fog. Any patrols would be just as vulnerable as I, unless they carried some sort of warder or immunity.

That's nonsense. There are no patrols. No one out here, but me. And the fog messing with my mind.

I bit my lip and pushed onward. More voices. Distinct this time. Orders. "Find the intruder." Right behind me. I dropped to my knees, awaiting a kick in the side or a blow to the head that never came.

Just the fog. But what if it weren't just the fog?

Waiting was pointless. If there were patrols, they'd find me. Better to be caught on the move than curled up in a whimpering ball. I forced myself to stand and proceeded on wobbly legs.

The buzzing grew louder. Covering my ears made no difference, as if the sound was inside my head, drowning out my thoughts. "This isn't real!" I shouted. My brain itched. Visions of falling into the sea filled my mind.

I dropped to my knees and crawled along the trail. One hand in front of the other. By now I must be nearing the top. I imagined I was a hundred steps (crawls?) from the summit. I cleared my mind of all other thoughts and counted down from one hundred. A hundred more steps to sunlight.

Ninety...Eighty-nine...Eighty-eight...

Could I stand and sprint to the top? But what if I tripped and dashed myself on the rocks?

Sixty-six...Sixty-five...Sixty-four...

I was hyperventilating. Couldn't catch my breath. My hands were tingling and my head d izzy...

Nineteen...Eighteen...Seventeen...

Muscles cramping. So close now.

Two...One...Zero...

Still in the fog.

Can't stop now. Made it one hundred steps. I can make it a hundred more.

I counted up...One...Two...Three...

Lost track of the switchbacks. What if I'm nowhere near the top?

Twenty-one...Twenty-two...Twenty-three...

So thirsty, but I don't want to stop, can't stop. Not even for a drink. Do I have any water left?

Forty-five...Forty-six...Forty-se—

The sun!

The big beautiful yellow ball of life shone down on me.

I dragged the rest of my body out of the fog and closed my eyes to the sounds of twittering birds.

***

By the time I trudged down the hill and into Mejica (no wagons heading to market), the sun had set. A shower at the rooming house rejuvenated me, and my head was clear from the effects of the fog. I visited the telegraph office at the rail station, sending a message to the cultural attaché who would pass it along to Rowe and Mehan:

Weather uncooperative with bird watching. Another attempt tomorrow.

What that attempt would be, I had no idea. I doubted my invocation of the weather would clue them in that the Ramorians had tempestarii. That would be news I'd have to deliver in person.

On my way back to the rooming house, I chanced to see two Ramorian sailors in their spiffy sapphire-blue uniforms. I followed them to a local tavern.

The establishment was your standard dive, with plenty of enlisted mixed in with rough-looking civilians. The waitress who took my order looked like she could arm-wrestle a bear. And win! From my corner table, I slurped watery soup, sipped stale beer, and watched the sailors and locals flirt, dance, and play darts.

After my meal, I exited the establishment and wandered about the street, ambling in a not-so-straight line and doing a passable imitation of a drunk. Keeping to the shadows, I followed a pair of sailors leaving a different bar, I tracked them to the naval base. The gate guard didn't raise his eyes when they passed through the entrance.

I had the germ of an idea.

***

The next morning, after a breakfast of stiff bread and passable coffee at the rooming house, I returned to the naval base. I rested on a bench across from the entrance gate, pretending to read *Migratory Birds*, and observed the same cavalier attitude toward security. Civilians were stopped, required to produce identity documents and roughly searched. But anyone in uniform didn't rate a second look.

After a couple of hours of surveillance, I moved on, scouting the base perimeter from a road that ran parallel. A ten-foot-high fence surrounded the base with razor wire strung on top. Trees and shrubs were cleared, leaving a twenty-foot gap between any covering and the fence.

As I passed by a string of shops on the opposite side of the road from the base, a gunshot rang out. Four cats scampered out the entrance of the butcher's shop. Three holding chicken legs in their mouths. The fourth urging them to "Run, mates, run!"

The butcher, a bald overweight man, emerged from his shop with shotgun in hand. He raised the weapon and took aim at the fleeing felines. I contrived to stumble into him, causing the butcher to drop the gun.

"Pardon, sir, but do you know the way to the rail station? I seem to have lost my way."

"You blithering idiot! Because of you those thieves got away." He reached down and retrieved his weapon.

"Those delightful pussy cats?"

"Thieves and bandits. All of them."

"You have my apologies, sir." I bowed my head. "Now, about the rail station?"

He looked at my clothes. "Damned foreigners." He stormed into his shop.

I wandered the perimeter for another hour, not learning anything new. Late in afternoon I headed to the train station and scanned the crowd for a familiar face. My young friend, the pickpocket, was plying his trade. He slipped his hand out of a lady's handbag. I locked onto his wrist.

"Pardon me, Madam. But I believe you dropped your change purse."

At the sight of the red and green item in the boy's hand, she exclaimed, "Oh, my!"

"My son saw it fall to the ground."

She smiled. "Such a good boy." She took the purse from his hand. "Let me give you a reward." She fished around for a coin.

I held up my hand. "Not necessary, Madam. Good deeds are their own reward." I tipped my cap. "Good day." I yanked the boy by the arm. "Come along, Son."

Away from the crowd, he spoke, "That's a pretty scabby trick. And what's with declining the reward? *Good deeds are their own reward.* Pfft." He spit.

"Here." I handed him a silver libra.

"What's this?"

"Your reward."

He eyed me suspiciously. "What's the angle?"

"I want to hire you."

He shook his head. "Don't need the work. I do all right."

"Yes, you do." I reached into his jacket pocket and pulled out three wallets.

"Give them back. Those are mine."

I opened one and slid out a Metalsmith's Guild ID. "Really? You're Mr. Joslin? Perhaps a constable could help us locate the owners of the other wallets."

"Why are you doing this? I gave you your money back."

"Correction. I caught you."

The boy shrugged. "Whatever."

"Now, about this job. I'll pay you five more libras."

"Ten."

"Seven. That's final."

"Seven and give me the loot back."

"Deal." I handed over the wallets.

"Where's my libras?"

"You get paid when the job's done."

"And what's the job."

"Stealing wallets."

"That's daft. You're paying me for what I already do."

"I need you to take one particular wallet."

"Whose?"

"I'll let you know when I do. Come along."

We walked from the station to the tavern from last night and waited at a spot up the road in the direction of the base. Sailors straggled by, mostly in twos or threes, occasionally by themselves. But none of the singletons were right.

The boy frowned and crossed his arms. "I can't spend the whole evening wasting time here. I need to work."

"I'm paying you."

"I haven't seen any money."

"Just wait and I—"

A sole sailor ambled down the street. The right height and bulk.

I nodded in the sailor's direction. "That's the one. The blonde sailor."

"Just nick his wallet? That's it?"

"There's a little more."

"What?"

"I need him to realize you took his wallet."

"That's not the point of this."

"You take his wallet. But let him see you. Chase you. Down the street and into that alley, next to the apothecary's shop. I'll be waiting. You get him there and I'll take care of the rest. Then you get your seven libras.

"Ten."

"The deal was for seven."

The boy frowned. "You want me to nick a sailor and let him chase me? Price is ten."

"Okay, ten. Give me a minute to get to the alley before you do your bit."

The boy grinned, and I hustled off to the alley. I grabbed a loose board and positioned myself behind a pile of crates. I found a gap that allowed me to watch the end of the alley.

Approaching footsteps. The kid rounded the alley corner at full speed. The sailor a few paces behind. "Stop, you delinquent!"

The boy sped past. I swung the board, my timing was perfect, and struck the sailor head on.

He dropped to the ground, unconscious, his nose broken, and blood dripping down his face. I frowned. Just a couple of years older than the pickpocket, probably a draftee. This kid didn't ask to get mixed up in international power politics and espionage. And now his face was ruined. That would be a small price to pay, if this mission, prevented a war.

But why was *this* kid the one who got stuck with the bill?

The boy jogged up, panting. "Wow, you really decked him."

The time for remorse was over. "C'mon and help me move him. He's a big fellow."

We dragged the sailor behind the crates. I removed his uniform.

"Hullo, what are you doing?" asked the boy.

"I need his clothes."

"Can I have his shoes?"

"No."

"What about my twenty libras?"

"The deal was ten. You'll get them once I'm in uniform and he's tied up." I made the right choice. The uniform was snug but fit. I stuffed my clothes into the knapsack and used a stretch of rope to tie up the sailor. "Here's your pay." I dropped two fivers into the boy's outstretched hand.

"Twenty!"

"The deal was for ten."

"That's before you laid him out. I go to the constable, you have plenty of trouble. Twenty's a steal for whatever your scheme is."

"Fine." I reached into my knapsack, pulled out a tenner and flipped it to the kid. "Now skedaddle."

The kid snatched the coin out of the air, darted down the alley, and disappeared around the corner.

I hid my knapsack in a crate. Couldn't go back to the rooming house dressed as a sailor. I wandered toward the base with the cap low over my eyes. I dawdled outside the view of the entrance gate, window shopping. A couple of sailors headed back into the base. I scampered across the road and followed ten steps behind.

They passed through the front gate with a smile and a wave to the guard. Avoiding eye contact, I raised my hand in a half-hearted wave. The guard didn't even look up.

The enchanted fog may have been a master stroke, but the rest of Ramorian security was sloppy at best.

No one paid me any mind. I strolled by the barracks, giving the occasional salute. I passed what looked to be the officer's quarters and an armory on the way to the docks.

The fog covered the mountain and the bay's entrance to the sea but didn't cover the actual base. That made sense. No one could do their jobs if they couldn't see. Plus, they'd be driven insane by fear and anxiety.

But if the base itself wasn't in the fog, why did our clairvoyants only see gray? Magic makes my head hurt.

I turned the corner around a storehouse and g— Holy Hell! Ironclads!

That's what the Ramorians didn't want anyone to see. Nobody had an inkling their technology advanced this far. Between this and their weather manipulation, Ramoria could provide quite an unpleasant surprise for our navy if we were to encounter them.

Three ironclads, seemingly of the same class. Guards posted at the gangplanks for each ship. I walked along the main dock counting the guns on each ship. Two sets, bow and stern. Looked to be six-inchers.

I continued along the main dock to the east until stopped by a gate. Past the gate were some smaller wooden vessels. Revenue cutters, maybe. Nothing worthy of a deep-sea voyage. I'd seen what I needed to, time to go.

I walked back to the west. Shouts in front of me. Guards pointing in my direction. More guards to my left, running toward me. Their security wasn't *that* sloppy.

With the gate behind me, only one direction to go. I sprinted down the pier. The guard at the gangplank took notice and moved to block my way.

I slowed to a stop and saluted. He raised his hand to return the salute, and I sucker-punched him, dropping him to his knees. I dashed to the end of the pier. No boat, dinghy, or even a life preserver. Shots rang out. Bullets whizzed over my head. Kicking off my stolen shoes, I plunged head first into the black water.

Swimming to shore wasn't an option. They'd gun me down as soon as I surfaced. Diving deep and back under the pier, I grabbed a piling and followed it to the surface. While I hid beneath them, the guards gathered at the end of the pier.

"I'm think I got him," said one voice.

"Get some boats in the water and make sure. I want his body."

"Yes, Chief!"

A rumble of footsteps on the pier. No way to be sure if there was anyone on top. I held on to the piling while the black water chilled my bones. Ten minutes later a pair of rowboats passed by. I took a deep breath and pushed myself under the surface, coming up long enough to take another breath and resubmerge. The security forces aimlessly paddled for a couple of hours until night fell.

Lucky for me there was a double full moon. I swam across the bay toward a spit of land jutting out from the shore. From my memory of the map, that land was outside the base perimeter. I swam the breaststroke, silent but fast. No splashing, and it kept my head above water so I could see.

Hours in the water left my body numb. About midnight, I dragged myself ashore and laid on the sand, gasping for air, shivering from cold. But I shouldn't stay on the beach. With my remaining strength I scrambled to my feet, stumbling thirty or forty feet to the woods, where I found refuge in a thicket of bushes. I collapsed on the ground and closed my eyes.

***

I awoke, face down, to the twitter of songbirds. My stomach rumbled; hadn't eaten since yesterday's lunch. I spit dirt from my mouth. My body shivered, the wet navy uniform plastered to my skin. Sunlight filtered through the trees. Rising slowly, I stood on wobbly legs and used the sun and the shoreline to get my bearings. Based on my mental map I headed toward Mejica. I needed to get the telegraph station and notify the embassy about the ironclads.

For all the protection the cheap Ramorian naval socks provided, I might as well have been barefoot. With bleeding soles and stubbed toes, I stumbled through the forest for twenty minutes until chancing upon a cabin in a clearing. Smoke curled from the slanted chimney, and to the side a line of laundry hung drying out. A few coins jingled in my pocket. I hoped to negotiate the purchase of some dry clothes.

The cabin was built from sagging, mismatched logs. No porch, only bare dirt at the entry. The door hung misaligned in its frame. I knocked lightly, worried that I might bring the entire structure down. The door opened to a hunched old man with gray hair and a matching unkempt beard.

"What do you want?" He squinted at me with black eyes. "Do I know you?"

I bowed my head. "Pardon, sir. But I'm in a terrible fix. Could I buy some clothes and a pair of shoes?"

He frowned. "This isn't the tailor's or cobbler's. This is my home."

I waved my hand at the trees. "Not many shops around. I haven't got much money, but I need to get into something dry."

He squinted again, this time at my clothes. "Navy, huh? What are you doing all the way out here? Are you deserting?"

What was the right answer? Was he a patriotic citizen who'd have no truck with a man who shirked his duty? Or a freedom-loving subversive ready to help out a draftee in need? Impossible to read the old man's wrinkled and impassive face.

"Answer me!"

I smiled. "Just disoriented after a wild night with my mates. I need to get back to base."

He stood up a little straighter. "Lost my only son in the war. The Army and the Navy can both go to

Hell. And you can get off my land!" He slammed the door in my face.

The clothes on the line beckoned to me. The old man was shorter than I, but hunched over. If the fit weren't perfect, they'd at least be dry. And I'd leave him a coin or two. I grabbed a shirt and pants off the line and some heavy wool socks. I sat on a stump and squeezed into the pants. Couldn't button the shirt up all the way. I peeled off what was left of the Navy socks and rubbed my feet.

A shotgun blast struck the tree in front of me.

"Thief!" the old man yelled. He let the other barrel go; shot whizzed by me. I grabbed the wool socks and skedaddled into the woods, as his shouts faded away.

I didn't expect him to follow. Once I was a decent distance, I put on the thicker socks. A marginal improvement, but the going was still slow. No more houses or any signs of civilization. I'd keep going in this direction until I hit a road or a river.

Two hours after the cabin, I emerged from the woods to find a well-used road with plenty of wheel tracks. I headed west toward where Mejica should be. Fifteen minutes later a wagon pulled up alongside me.

"Can I get a ride into Mejica?" I said a silent prayer. I'd stolen from one civilian (never had a chance to leave payment for the clothes) and didn't want to have to assault another. But I would, if need be. Rowe and Mehan needed to be informed about the fleet and the tempestarii. I must get to the telegraph station.

The farmer shrugged. "One soldo."

That confirmed I was headed in the right direction. I fished in my pocket, grabbed a coin and tossed it to him. With his thumb he pointed to the back of the wagon. I clambered in and tried to make myself comfortable amongst the farmer's produce as we rumbled on our way. I checked my pockets. One libra and two soldos, not enough for a telegram. Would need to stop at the rooming house first. I spit on my hands and cleaned the cuts on my feet. I nibbled the brown kernels of a drought-stunted ear of corn.

The wagon rattled into town. I leapt when it slowed for a turn, heading for the telegraph station with a new idea. "I want to send a telegram COD," I told the clerk.

She motioned toward the machine. "Line's been down since last night."

An unfortunate coincidence.

"Can I give you the message and you send it when the line's back up?"

She nodded. "Sure." She handed me a pad and pen.

I wrote out: *Three gray owls sporting thick feathers. Weather still an issue. Michael McCarthy.* Then added the address of the embassy in care of the cultural attaché.

Rowe gave no code for ironclads. I hoped the two of them would puzzle it out in the event I didn't make it back. I handed the form to the clerk. She paid it no particular mind and placed it in the stack of outgoing messages.

Instead of the rooming house, I headed across town to the alley to retrieve my knapsack. My appearance and clothing earned some stares from the citizenry. When I reached the alley, the knapsack was gone. The juvenile cutpurse, no doubt. Next stop: the rooming house.

I approached the rooming house from across the street and saw the boy pickpocket sitting on the porch. Was he looking for another reward by selling me my knapsack?

The boy stood, pointed at me, and yelled. Two constables emerged from the rooming house. Should have figured on that. I turned and ran. A whistle blew. I forced my way through the crowd, knocking down random people in my path.

With my considerable head start, the constables weren't going to catch me, but where could I go? The train station was out. They'd catch me there for sure. I could try one of the roads out of town and hitch another wagon ride. But I was hundreds of versts from the embassy in Lavko with three coins in my pocket and the constabulary on my tail. With the boy's help they must have pieced together my activities and concluded I was the spy who breached the base's security. They weren't going to stop searching until they found me.

If they were smart about it, they'd check at the telegraph station. Ask the clerk if she'd seen anyone matching my description. Go through the pending telegrams. Couldn't count on the message getting through. I would have to deliver it myself. Only way to head off a potential war. I must find a way onto the train. They'd be watching the station. I didn't have enough money to buy a ticket. If I eluded the constables and boarded, I'd be found out by a conductor.

The stop outside town! On the journey from the capital, the train stopped to load and unload livestock. Maybe ten minutes travel time from the station.

I stopped running. The constables had lost track of me. No need to attract attention. I walked through town parallel to the track, with an eye out for authorities, but saw none. When the town ended and buildings gave way to fields, I followed the path beside the tracks. The brown fields gave way to woods on both sides of the track. A half-hour walk along the tracks brought me to a stockyard full of sheep, pigs, and cows.

I slowed my pace as I walked by the pens. Earned some suspicious looks from the ranch hands tending to the animals. Continued to follow the tracks until they curved around a bend. I slipped into the woods opposite the pens and backtracked to the stockyard. When the train arrived, no one in the stockyard would have a view of me. I'd slip aboard and be back in the capital in a few hours. Assuming the train headed to Lavko.

I dropped back into the woods out view of the tracks and sat down with my back propped up against a tree. I slid off the purloined socks. Blood oozed from my soles and my feet swelled. I rubbed, but it didn't help. I closed my eyes, counted backward from five hundred and drifted off.

***

The whine of the train whistle shook me from my slumber.

The sun was high overhead, noon or a bit later. I slipped the socks over my swollen feet and padded through the woods to the tracks.

I crouched and could see the underside of a ramp, animals being loaded. Sheep bleated. Pigs oinked. Cows mooed.

Cows! The fortuneteller said to follow the cows.

I crawled along ground peering under the cars until the unmistakable sight of cow legs came into view.

A glance in either direction revealed no conductors. I scrambled to the train, leapt, and grabbed hold of the metal rungs on the side of the boxcar. I climbed up the side, grimacing as my tender feet strained against the rusted metal. I hauled myself on top. Keeping my head down, I located the trap door and slipped inside. I half-way descended another set of metal rungs. The boxcar was filled with the overpowering stench of stale hay and manure. No ranch hands, just cows piling in the car. I hid in the shadows in the corner halfway up the rungs. I removed my shirt, slipped it through two rungs, wrapped the sleeves around my chest and tied a knot. With my feet propped up on a narrow shelf, I wedged myself into a stable but uncomfortable position. One preferable to being trampled by a two-ton heifer.

The last of the cows squeezed in and the boxcar's door slid shut. The train whistle sounded, and the car lurched forward. In a minute, we were racing down the tracks. Every bump jarred my aching body. But my position was secure, and I managed to half-sleep.

***

The train lurched to a stop, waking me from my insufficient slumber. The air was stuffy, the heat oppressive. I swallowed, but my mouth was dry. My hands and feet were numb; my muscles ached. I fumbled several times trying to untie the shirt-sleeve knot that held me in place. Sensation replaced the numbness, and I undid the knot. Climbing the metal rungs, my right calf cramped. Suppressing a cry, I flexed my leg, and climbed out of the car.

Clouds covered the stars and moons. A cool breeze blew and my lungs welcomed the fresh air. I recognized Central Station; I made it to Lavko! In my haste to climb down the rungs, my hand slipped, and I plummeted to the ground with a thud.

I didn't cry out, I couldn't. The wind was knocked out me. I writhed on the ground, gasping for air, muscles cramping.

A lantern shone in my eyes. "What do we have here?"

A man in a blue uniform. Constable or Railroad Security?

I tried to speak, but no words were forthcoming.

He knelt to inspect me. I tried to grab the lantern, and he brought his baton down on my arm hard.

"Arggh!" My voice and breath were back.

"Looks like another hobo tried to score a free ride."

I shook my head. "Just a little lost. Had too much to drink. Trying to find my way back to the hotel."

"Public intoxication is against the law."

I got on my knees. "Please. I just want to go to bed and sleep it off."

He shook his head. "Can't do that."

I stood up using the side of the car for balance. I took one slow step forward. If I could get close eno—

"No." He stepped back, the baton went into its sleeve and he pulled out a pistol.

"You're drunk and half-dressed. It's after curfew and you hitched a free ride. You've just earned a free night in the jail."

I forced a smile. "Look, I'm a wealthy man, perhaps we could come to some sort of agreement."

"Yes, wealthy men often hop trains and dress like vagrants. And attempted bribery of a government official is a felony. Now you're looking at hard time, fellow. Turn around and walk slowly toward the station."

I did as he asked. We trudged through the yard. When we neared the station, he said, "Head to the left, through the gate and out to the street."

I recognized the general store with the rancid cheese. "I don't suppose tha—"

"Quiet! One more word out of you and I'll save the judge the trouble of sentence."

Could going to the jail be the answer? If the telegraph line being down was a ruse, McCarthy would be on some watch list. Stick to the claim of being a drunken tourist and ask for help from the embassy? Or help from the embassy of one of our allies and have them get a message to Rowe?

On this mission all my instincts had been wrong. Every decision incorrect: The fog, the penetration of the base, even the old man who asked if I were a deserter. My luck was due to change. If on—

"Aieee!" screamed the constable. I turned to see him struggling, but it wasn't clear with what. The gun dropped from his hand. He swatted at his face and his chest. He shrieked again.

Something on his face. Small. Brown. A mouse!

He grabbed the mouse and flung it against the wall of a store. The body struck with a sickening thud. I charged the disoriented constable and struck him with a right cross. He staggered backward and collapsed on the ground. I grabbed his gun off the ground and followed a series of faint squeaks in the darkness to the mouse curled up in pain.

"Basilius!"

"We are even, Mr. Linn," he said between labored breaths.

"More than even, friend." I grabbed Basilius with my free hand and dashed through the empty streets to the embassy to prevent a war.

***

At the embassy gate the pair of MSCs took one look at me and laughed. The guard on the right said, "Sorry, pal. Embassy function tonight and you're most certainly not on the invitation list."

I didn't have time and wasn't in the mood for explanations. I leveled the constable's pistol at his head. "Here's my invitation."

He backed down immediately and stepped aside. I raced up the walk. MSCs are mostly for show. Not worried he'd chase after me, I tossed the gun in the bushes. I burst into the embassy and found the same bored duty clerk at the front desk from the day I received my assignment.

"I need a doctor."

"What's wrong? Mr. Linn, right? Are you injured?"

"Just get one. Now!"

She scampered off down the hallway.

I laid Basilius on the desk. He was unconscious, and his breathing shallow.

The clerk returned with the doctor, a colonel in his dress whites.

"What's the problem here?"

I pointed to Basilius. "He was flung against a wall. He's hurt bad. Help him."

The doctor took one look at Basilius and sniffed. "That's a mouse. I'm a doctor, not a veterinarian."

I stepped forward and poked my finger in his chest. "This mouse's survival is a matter of national security. You're a healer. Heal him. Or I'll see your next posting is in Ultima Thule."

He sighed. "I'll see what I can do." He began his examination.

"And his name is Basilius."

The doctor told the clerk, "Find the duty nurse and send her down to my office." He gathered up Basilius with both hands and disappeared down the hallway.

I collapsed in the chair and closed my eyes. I re-opened them when I heard the clerk return.

"I need to see Rowe."

"Who?"

"Don't play games. Major Rowe and Mehan."

"They're at the ball. Whatever it is I'm sure it can wait. Maybe you'd like to clean up first?"

I was half-naked, covered in dirt and smelled like a cow pasture, but I'd made it to the embassy. The Ramorians' secret was out. My report could wait thirty minutes or an hour. "Yeah, that's probably a good idea. And can you rustle up some food? I haven't eaten in a day and a half."

***

With a full stomach, scrubbed skin, and fresh clothes, I felt like a new man. I stopped by the doctor's office to check on Basilius.

"You want me to save his life? Don't bother me!" the colonel roared.

Back at the front desk I asked, "Any word from Rowe?"

The clerk shook her head.

"Why don't I go see him? Where's the function?"

"The main ballroom. It's on the second floor down the r—"

"I'm sure I can find it."

The ballroom was filled with men in dress uniforms or stuffed into tuxedos and ladies in dazzling gowns. A full orchestra played while dancers waltzed. I skirted the perimeter looking for Rowe. He wasn't at any of the tables, but I spotted him on the dance floor, waltzing with a statuesque redhead in a gravity-defying turquoise gown.

When he turned in my direction, I waved. He smiled in return and kept waltzing. When the music ended, the dancers applauded. I motioned to

Rowe, he ignored me, paired up with a new partner (Mehan!) and began to dance.

I marched across the dance floor dodging twirling couples, right up to the pair. "Rowe! I've got the report on Corvis Bay."

Rowe and Mehan stopped dancing.

"Can't you see we're busy?" He glanced at Mehan.

I grabbed him by the shoulder and shook him. "My report is urgent. I need to be debriefed."

He removed my hands from his person. "Linn, it doesn't matter. The treaty has been signed."

"What treaty?"

The orchestra stopped playing. The other dancers gathered around us.

"We have a new alliance with Ramoria. With their new ironclads combined with our fleet we will rule the seas."

"Ironclads? You know? When did this happen?"

"Two days ago," said Mehan. "I did say in the briefing that events were moving rapidly. The ball is a celebration of our new alliance."

"Two days? That's the day I departed. You said I'd get a recall notice as soon as the fleet was located."

"Sorry." She shrugged. "We've all been busy."

"*Very* busy, Linn." Rowe sighed. "And now if you could let us celebrate the fruit of our efforts." He made a shooing motion with his hand.

The smug bastard.

I clipped Rowe with a left hook, sending him sprawling to the floor. I piled on top of him and rained a dozen blows upon his head before embassy security wrestled me away.

***

Since Rowe and I were Reservists, laying him out was more than simple assault. It earned me a Chapter Sixty-Three hearing. In wartime, I could have been shot. In peacetime, a guilty verdict could land me up to twenty years hard labor in the adamantium mines. The combination of my service record, my obstinate court-martial barrister, and a desire from the higher ups to sweep the incident under the rug enabled me to plead out to time served: two months in the brig on bread and water.

I cashed out my pension (got 25%) and said good-bye to home and the service. Between the alliance with Ramoria and Rowe's promotion to section chief (running the Northwest desk) I wasn't feeling too hopeful about our nation's future.

I drifted for a while before landing in The Seven Isles. Politically neutral and so far off the shipping lanes as to be strategically insignificant, they boasted no natural resources except an overabundance of warm weather and shapely natives with an aversion to clothes.

Most tourists who make it to the Seven Isles stay on the Big Island. Only the adventurous traveled to Lentern, the smallest and most distant of the seven. On the west coast of Lentern sat the port town of Dauphus, where I procured a fishing boat with my buyout.

That colonel at the embassy was quite the miracle worker. He fixed Basilius up like new. I arranged to sneak him out of Ramoria, which is a whole other adventure. Now he lives with me on the boat. An orchard grows behind the marina. From time-to-time, I trade some of our catch for all the fresh pears and apples Basilius can eat.

Walk all the way to the far end of the docks to the last slip in the marina. That's where you'll find us. The name of our boat is *The Last Mission*.

THE END

About the Author

James Blakey lives in the Shenandoah Valley where he writes mostly full-time. He's a three-time finalist for the Short Mystery Fiction Society's Derringer Award, winning in 2019 for his story "The Bicycle Thief." He leads critique groups in Harrisonburg, Charlottesville, and Shenandoah County. His paranormal thriller SUPERSTITION will be published by City Owl Press in the fall of 2024. When James isn't writing, he's on the hiking trail—he's climbed forty of the fifty US state high points—or bike-camping his way up and down the East Coast.

Visit JamesBlakeyWrites.com, sign up for my newsletter, and receive a free copy of "Do Not Pass Go..." Sleuthsayers.org called it one of their "Best of the Best."

Follow me on social media:

Twitter/X – @JamesWBlakey
Instagram – @JamesBlakeyAuthor
Facebook – @JamesWBlakey

If you enjoyed this collection, please leave a review at your favorite book retailer.

www.ingramcontent.com/pod-product-compliance
Lightning Source LLC
Chambersburg PA
CBHW021558310726
48972CB00003B/853